Mistress Karin

Constance Pennington Smythe
Copyright © 2008
ISBN 978-1-934446-11-9
Cover Art by VIPER

Published by
Romance Divine LLC
Find us on the
World Wide Web at
www.romancedivine.com

Second Edition
Previously Published as: Mistress Karin
ISBN 978-1-60054-052-X

For My Lovely Girls

You Know Who You Are

Mistress Karin

by

Constance Pennington Smythe

One

It began as it did every morning.

Karin Calloway burrowed into the covers and nestled her head deeper into the pillow. She was awake now, and felt the hands gently massaging her feet. Then she felt the tongue, Suzette's tongue, delicately licking the soles. They were soft loving licks, from the ball of the foot to the heel. Suzette's tongue flattened itself over her Mistress's foot, steadily moving just the way she had been trained. While she licked one foot, her hands gently massaged the other.

Karin stretched and sighed. *Twenty more minutes*, she thought. She'd give herself twenty minutes since she didn't have to be at the office early today. And after all, she owned what was once 'his' e company.

Because she had been well trained, Suzette continued her ministrations. This was her first morning service to her Mistress, to kneel naked at the foot of Mistress's bed and wake her with a foot rub. Routine was the hallmark of Suzette's life. She never had to think of her next action; her's was an orderly and well regimented existence. She was trained to perform exacting service.

Fifteen minutes later, Suzette saw Karin stretch and spread her legs, and responded immediately to this non-verbal command. Gently, she climbed onto the bed and carefully positioned herself at Mistress's bottom, her pink tongue delicately descending into the puckered opening.

Satisfied with the anal foreplay, Karin flexed her bottom, a silent command for Suzette to go deeper. Karin sighed. *A Mistress doesn't need words when her slave is properly trained,* she thought. *Discipline and rigorous training are all they need...and a desire to serve.* Suzette possessed the desire to serve, Karin provided the training, and now it was paying off. She wasn't exactly sure what kind of life Suzette now had, and she didn't really care. Karin was getting exactly what she wanted and that was really all that mattered.

"Deeper!" Karin said. She spread her legs wider, opening herself more as Suzette strained to burrow her face even deeper into her Mistress's pink cleft.

"Wiggle it about in there, don't just stick it in."
"Ah, yes, that's better, um...yes."

After another five minutes, and finally satisfied, Karin snapped her fingers.

Suzette moved quickly to take up a kneeling position on the floor by Mistress's side of the bed, her hands demurely clasped behind her back, her body erect, eyes cast down to the floor.

Karin rose from her bed and stood before Suzette. With a beautifully manicured nail she lifted Suzette's chin. The hand suddenly came away from the chin and delivered a stinging slap. Suzette flinched but did not break position. Karin smiled; the benefits of training included lots of slapping. She struck Suzette again. SLAP!

"Your tongue in my ass is one of the greatest privileges you can receive." SLAP! Suzette's face was getting red. "When you are allowed to tongue my ass," ...SLAP... "you need to do it like it's the most important thing in your life." SLAP!

Suzette remained upright, to break position during discipline always invited more of the same. But her face stung, and she shook uncontrollably as tears began to form.

Karin reached down and grabbed a nipple between her long, blood-red nails. As she pinched and twisted, Suzette squirmed internally with the pain, but did not flinch.

Karin laughed. "You little slut," she chided, noticing Suzette's growing erection. With that she planted a foot on Suzette's chest and pushed her to the floor. "Get my slippers."

Suzette crawled away to fetch the slippers, bringing them back in her mouth.

Karin took the slippers, checking them for tooth marks. She nodded approvingly, "Yes my little bitch, you're learning." She dropped the slippers on the floor and Suzette lovingly helped her into them.

Kneeling before her Mistress, Suzette felt Karin's mocking disdain. Cowering, she knelt with her hands planted firmly, palms down, on the carpet.

Karin moved her foot slowly, lightly dragging the sole of the shoe over Suzette's splayed fingers. Gradually, she applied more pressure. Because she knew her slave paid heed to the increasing pain, she wouldn't notice Karin reaching for the riding crop on the bedside table.

Suzette didn't see Karin pick up the crop, focused instead on the pain being inflicted on her hand. A sore hand would be no excuse for failing to perform Mistress's long list of the day's demanding chores.

With increasing pressure, Karin ground her shoe into Suzette's hand. She brought the crop down on Suzette's ass in a sudden and brutal attack. SMACK! Suzette flinched and cried out. "I do enjoy our little morning sessions," laughed Karin, "don't you?"

"If it pleases Mistress," whimpered Suzette.

"I do whatever pleases me, whenever I want." The crop came down again. SMACK! Karin gave Suzette's hand a final step and backed away. "Go prepare my morning bath."

As Suzette crawled to the bathroom to do her Mistress' bidding, she heard Karin's mocking voice. "My little slut, maybe if you're good this morning I'll piss in your oatmeal."

While Karin bathed, Suzette changed into her uniform. The daily maid outfit was usually the same unless Mistress directed otherwise. Karin preferred Suzette wear a garter belt with black seamed stockings and no panties so that she, or any of her guests, could grope Suzette at their leisure.

For today, Mistress selected a heavily boned and underwired bra, with rather large breast inserts, giving Suzette that ridiculous and slutty look befitting her position. A black maid's dress with white lace trim and apron went over the undergarments. Accessories included a black and white lace choker and white maid's cap. For morning and afternoon duties, black patent four inch stiletto heels were worn. Depending on the evening's activities the heels would increase to five inch or six inches. Suitably attired and having accomplished her kitchen duties, Suzette knocked on the bathroom door.

"In," Karin commanded. Suzette entered and curtsied sloppily, her attention focused on not spilling the juice in the glass. She carefully placed the glass on the ledge of the tub and turned slowly to be inspected.

When Karin casually placed two fingers to her lips Suzette pulled the pack of cigarettes and a lighter from her apron pocket and placed the nearby ashtray next to the juice.

When the cigarette was lit, Karin blew a long stream of smoke into Suzette's face. With a gesture indicating boredom, she dismissed her and watched Suzette back demurely out of the room. Karin sank into the warm bath and savored her first cigarette of the day. Such pampering, and to think of all the years she wasted as a typical wife. Hers was now a life of luxury. She reveled in her role as the spoiled bitch and intended not to waste another minute on anything that wasn't solely for her pleasure or amusement.

The very thought of such endless hedonistic pleasures made her sex tingle. She dropped the cigarette in the ashtray, her hands disappearing into the warm soapy water. She sought out those folds of skin that lay between her legs, stroking herself lovingly, feeling the sensations of the caresses in the warm water. With her left hand she spread herself and let the fingers of her right find their way inside. Hungrily she touched and stroked her wet, hot sex. *Mmm, it's good to be me, a spoiled and pampered bitch who gets what she wants. It's good to be me.*

She finished her bath and reached for the crystal bell. A casual observer might think Karin collected bells, as they were found all over the house, but the bells were a convenience and a symbol of her power. Suzette had been painstakingly trained to respond to the bells. Karin gave the bell two quick shakes. Within seconds, she heard the clicking of Suzette's heels as she made her way toward Mistress's bath.

Entering properly and offering heartfelt respect, Suzette took a large, luxurious towel and wrapped it around her Mistress. She grabbed another towel and dropped to her knees to dry Karin's legs and feet. When the feet were dry Suzette placed the high-heeled slippers on Karin's feet, as Mistress casually discarded the towel to the floor for her maid to tend later.

Suzette crawled to the bathroom door and knelt on the hard, tile floor. As Karin strode from the bathroom, she managed to step on each of Suzette's hands without breaking her stride or to peer down and aim her steps. Suzette winced as Karin's spiked heels mauled her hands but uttered no cry. To complain would be to invite a punishment much worse than that momentary discomfort.

Karin delighted in these episodes. *Is it my imagination or can I really feel the way the flesh and knuckles compress under the hard plastic platform soles and spiked heels? Mmmmm...such a delicious suffering and torment to inflict.*

"My gray suit with the pink shell and my gray

pumps," Suzette heard from the bedroom.

"Yes, Mistress."

Suzette went to the closet and removed Karin's gray skirt and jacket and the soft, silk, pink shell. She carefully took the exquisite shoes from their box. Suzette carried the items to Karin's dressing table and hung the suit on the nearby rack. When she finished with this task she applied a moisturizing lotion to Karin's back and shoulders.

Karin hung her head, sighed and relaxed. A skilled masseuse taught Suzette to perform these services. The masseuse was a stern woman and the training regimen rather harsh, but Suzette learned her lessons well. In return, Suzette kept the masseuse's house clean and performed other domestic and "personal" chores. *It was a month well spent* mused Karin. Sublimely moisturized and satiated Karin snapped her fingers.

Suzette immediately stopped and moved to stand beside her Mistress, head hung submissively, hands clasped behind her back, feet together, her "waiting" position.

Except for her clear spike heels, Karin was naked, a pleasure she indulged in regularly. It was fun, enticing Suzette with pleasures she would seldom enjoy. Karin reached under Suzette's dress and lightly stroked the cock, feeling the tremors that ran through her maid's flesh. *No matter how much you punish them, humiliate them and degrade them, they still long for and respond to that touch.* Karin loved teasing her maid and she was a master at her craft.

"Toast, two pieces," she murmured as she tormented the cock with her fingernails.

"Yes, Mistress."

"Coffee." Her fingernail traced a circle around the sensitive head of the cock. Suzette's knees buckled, bringing a smile to Karin's face. "An egg in one of the Egg Coddler cups." Karin began to pinch the head of the cock between her dagger-like nails. *Such a fine line between pleasure and pain.* She pinched harder.

"Please, Mistress," begged Suzette.

Karin yanked on the cock, pulling Suzette down. With her free hand she slapped Suzette across the face.

"Did I give you permission to speak?" she yelled. Her grip on the cock tightened.

"No, Mistress."

"You've got a rough little mouth, you bitch. You better clean up your act or I'll beat you so bad you won't sit for the next three days."

"Yes, Mistress."

"Maybe we need to soften up your mouth a bit. Hmmm, let's see what we have," Karin purred as she looked over her makeup table. With her wicked smile, she continued, "Yes, yes, stick out your tongue."

Suzette complied and Karin roughly grabbed it between her fingernails, pulling hard as she picked up a container of baby powder. "This should soften up that rough little mouth of yours."

Suzette's eyes widened with fear. She tried to shake her head in a desperate plea. "Plthh, nahh, plth," Suzette mumbled, her tongue still in Karin's grasp.

"I'm sorry dear, but I really can't understand what

you're trying to say." Karin smiled now, enjoying herself. She stretched the wet, pink tongue and lightly dusted it with the baby powder. Suzette made horrible noises and tears formed in her eyes. Karin simply laughed, released Suzette's tongue and pushed her away. "Close that mouth and keep it closed."

Suzette retreated and resumed her position, making horrible faces and gagging sounds. "Don't you dare throw up on my fine Turkish rug! If you do, you'll lick up every drop." Karin let Suzette stand and suffer for a few moments while she laughed and mocked her. "All right, go and finish my breakfast."

Suzette curtsied, turned and walked away.

Karin's eyes followed her with a look of disgust. *Those curtsies were sloppy; we'll have to work on those some more.*

When Karin came downstairs she found Suzette standing beside the impeccably set dining room table. Breakfast was prepared exactly as Karin had ordered. Suzette pulled out the chair for her Mistress then poured the coffee. When the cup was full, Suzette returned to her submissive position.

Karin picked up the morning paper to peruse the business section while she ate in silence. When she was finished eating, she put two fingers to her lips and Suzette responded with the obligatory cigarette. Her breakfast finished, Karin placed her plate on the floor.

Suzette dropped to her hands and knees, crawled to the plate and licked it clean of the leftovers while her Mistress read her newspaper and smoked. She continued until the tinkling bell prompted her next task, when she arose and cleared the table. She poured her Mistress a last cup of coffee before taking the dirty dishes to the kitchen.

Karin was oblivious to Suzette's efforts. *After all, the creature is only doing what she was trained to do, right?*

When Karin entered the kitchen Suzette curtsied to her Mistress who absently nodded. Suzette went to the center of the room and knelt on the hard, cold kitchen tile.

Karin took the blender, filled it with cold water, poured in some oatmeal and pushed the "Stir" switch. She turned to face her kneeling maid and put another cigarette in her holder. The blender churned while Karin smoked. "I may be bringing someone home tonight. If so, I'll call and give you instructions." Casually, she knocked the cigarette ash into the blender. "You have your list of chores for today and I'll expect them to be complete when I get home." She tapped more ash into the blender, then bent over and spit, her drool consumed in the whirling vortex. "I've scheduled you an appointment with Trudi, today, at one. Be sure and behave."

She smoked in silence for a moment and flicked more ash into the blender. Finally she reached over and turned off the appliance, the room lapsing into momentary silence. Blender in one hand, she walked towards Suzette, circling her prey. The only sound in the room was the clicking of her heels. Taking her time, she walked around the kitchen and slowly poured the cold, disgusting porridge on the floor. "I do hope you appreciate that I have taken the time to prepare your breakfast. And I want you to lick up each and every drop. Remember, the cameras will be on, and I, and my secretary, can monitor you on our computers at work." Karin finished her walk, admiring the slimy trail of gruel on the floor. She dropped the empty blender in the sink and walked to the front door.

Suzette rose to fetch Karin's coat and briefcase, and found Karin touching up her lipstick at the mirror by the front door.

Karin took the final drag on her cigarette, knocked the ash to the tile floor and placed the holder in a nearby ashtray. She allowed Suzette to help with her coat then pointed a finger towards the floor. *Words aren't required when they are properly trained.*

Suzette dropped to her knees to kiss the toes of Mistress's shoes, paused for a moment, and then licked up the cigarette ash.

Karin laughed. "Well, well, my little bitch, it seems that husbands can be trained. I'll inspect your work this evening; do a good job." With that she turned and left.

Suzette knew that the cameras were on and that Mistress's secretary was monitoring them as Karin drove to the office. Resignedly, she crawled into the kitchen to lick up the mess, her breakfast, left by Mistress Karin.

All in all it had been a typical morning for both of them.

"YES MS. CALLOWAY, I HAVE HER ON THE MONI-
TOR. SHE FINISHED LICKING UP ALL OF HER BREAK-
FAST. OH AND I LOVE THE NEW RUMBA PANTIES
WITH THE LACE RUFFLES THAT YOU HAVE HER
WEARING.

"YES, YOU HAVE THE TOMLINSON MEETING AT
TEN-THIRTY AND A LUNCHEON DATE AT ONE; I MADE
YOUR RESERVATIONS.

"CERTAINLY I CAN STOP BY AND CHECK ON
SUZETTE ON MY WAY HOME. OF COURSE I'LL RECORD
SUZETTE'S DANCE PRACTICE THIS AFTERNOON. MY
GIRLFRIENDS GET A KICK OUT OF WATCHING A MALE
BEING TURNED INTO AN EROTIC DANCER. WE CAN'T
WAIT TO SEE HER PERFORM IN FRONT OF A MAN."

Two

Timing was everything. Karin needed to pick the right time to catch him off guard; Steven would be most surprised, confused, and helpless in those first critical moments. They were sitting on the couch watching TV, reading, relaxing, when she began his descent into slavery and submission.

"Do you really want to be my love slave?" she asked.

"Sure," he stammered. "Haven't - uh - I - uh, always said so?" He was startled and confused.

Karin gave him a long and seductive stare. The silence made him nervous and she smiled as he nervously licked his lips. "Do you know what that means?"

"Yea, it - it means I do everything to please you, obey you completely, uh - that kind of thing." He said it as more of a question, hoping to get some reassurance. Her timing had been perfect; he definitely was taken aback by my statement.

"Yes, it means that and so much more. Are you ready to submit totally to me, to obey me without question, to suffer for me, to submit to every pain and humiliation I choose for you?" She saw a growing hard-on and the flush on his face; he was clearly excited.

Steven slid off the couch and dropped to his knees before her, his head bowed so his eyes were on the floor. "Yes," he said, "I will be your love slave and submit to you."

Going down on his knees had been a good move on his part as Karin was ready to kick him off the couch. *A slave's place is on the floor, not on my furniture. Maybe he thought this was going to be some sort of a game that ends at bed-time. This is no game.* They had played at this before, now she intended to push the limit, and at the same time enjoy an indulgent life of pampered luxury. *Does he really want to serve me, to worship me, to suffer for my pleasure, to wait on me hand and foot? We'll see.*

"Strip!" she commanded. When he didn't move fast enough she reached out and slapped his face, not hard enough to do damage, but a stinging blow that hurt. "Faster!" She laughed as he struggled to get out of his clothes while remaining on his knees.

When he was finally naked she ordered him to kneel with his hands clasped behind his neck, and made him put his elbows back as far as possible. This exposed his tender nipples and underarms. His eyes remained focused on the floor.

Karin reached forward and tormented his nipples, pinching, and scratching them with her long sharp nails. By design she had put new ones on the day before, long, sharp ones, painted a fiery red. When she asked if he liked them she'd received the usual bored-male, "Oh yea," response. But now his cock was rock-hard, his male biology sending her all the visual clues she needed.

"Let's go over the rules," she said. "Number one: You speak only when spoken to and address me as Mistress." She continued her nipple torment.

"Number two: You will remain naked at all times and wear only the clothes I direct you to wear.

"Number three: You will obey my commands immediately and to my complete satisfaction. Your only thought is to serve me.

"Number four: Any infraction will result in punishments of my choosing. I may also choose to punish you just because it pleases me to do so." She increased her nipple torment, pinching and twisting his little buds. His cock started to ooze pre-cum; exactly what she wanted, a link between his pain and pleasure.

"Number five: You are not allowed to have an orgasm except at my command. Your one goal is to please me; your pleasure means nothing. Any unauthorized orgasms will result in punishment, plus you will lick up your mess." She wiped the pre-cum from his cock and held her cum-soaked finger to his lips. "Open wide," she taunted. He was almost beside himself, yet he did it.

"Suck it all you little bitch, and be sure you swallow." While he sucked her cum-soaked finger, she dug the nails of her other hand into his nipple. He gagged as he swallowed.

"Get used to it slut, until you get that cock of yours under control you'll eat a lot of it. It's pay-back time for all those years of women having to swallow from disgusting blow jobs. I intend to teach you to appreciate what it is to be a woman, and to respect and yield to superior women."

She gave each of his nipples a final pinch and then

sat back on the couch. It all may have been a bit too intense for him, and she allowed him a minute to regain his composure. Karin stood and walked toward the bedroom. "Follow me on your hands and knees."

He crawled behind, silent and submissive. In the bedroom she positioned him in the middle of the floor, on his hands and knees, placing her riding crop on the floor before him. She set a kitchen timer for thirty minutes.

"You've seen how I can be. It's time for you to decide. You may choose to continue to be my slave and follow my rules. If that's your choice, then wait until timer goes off and crawl to me with the crop in your mouth. If you choose not to be my slave - well, then you can leave the room at any time and nothing more about this matter will be discussed. If you choose to serve me, only I will know when you will be required to do so. You may spend every minute outside of work for a week as my slave, or weeks may go by without your serving me. Only I will know; and when I say to serve you must obey instantly. Do you understand?"

"Yes, Mistress," he replied.

She looked at the timer. "You have twenty eight minutes to think about it." As she left the room, she noticed his cock was still leaking pre-cum on her beautiful wood floors. *He'll pay for that!*

While she waited Karin marveled at how easy it had been. *I wondered how far either of us will go? What's his capacity for pain and humiliation? How much pleasure and luxury can I take? Probably a lot; let's see, no more dusting, vacuuming, laundry. I can have the sheets washed weekly, the bed made daily, and the bathroom and kitchen floors cleaned weekly, on his hands and knees for a thorough job! Everything done when I want it, the way I want it. Does he really gain excitement from serving me? Well, we'll see, won't we?* Karin amused herself with a magazine while her slave pondered his fate on his hands and knees.

After fifteen minutes she knew the only way he would come out of that room was on his hands and knees with a riding crop in his mouth. Sure enough, Karin heard the 'ding' of the timer and he came crawling out and stopped at her feet.

"So you've decided to be my slave?"

"Yes, Mistress," his response muffled by the crop he carried so lovingly in his mouth.

She took the crop from his mouth. "Very well, if at any time you can no longer bear the pain or humiliation you must say, 'I yield'. Repeat it."

"I yield," he said.

Reaching down she wiped more cum from his cock. She held her finger to his lips and smiled as he took it into his mouth. His sucking was half-hearted and she struck him with the crop. "If I offer you your own cum you must eat it, and appreciate it as the gift that it is, coming from your Mistress. Show me how much you enjoy it!" He tried harder but she struck him again.

When he was finished she led him back to the bedroom and made him lick up his cum from the wood floor. To hurry him on she used the crop on his bare ass, leaving red welts. *Tomorrow he'll be thinking of me every time he sits down.*

She returned to the living room, her dutiful slave crawling behind. Karin curled up on the couch while

Steven massaged her feet. He'd always liked to rub and lick her feet and did it often. Well, she liked it too, and Karin had the feeling that he would tire of it long before she did. Tonight she made him do it for ninety minutes, longer than he'd ever done it before. She gave him directions, "Lick the sole, rub the other one, lick in between my toes, now the other one, suck the toes, lick the heel, use your lips to massage my sole."

She was relentless and demanding; whenever he slacked off or seemed inattentive she used the crop on his back. After ninety minutes of foot worshipping she was ready for bed. Karin made her slave dress her for bed. She made him kneel at the side of the bed as she teasingly brought herself to orgasm with a vibrator while he could only watch, frustrated. Finally fully satisfied, Karin was ready for sleep. "Time for bed," she taunted.

As he started to get into bed she laughed, "Not for you. I want the refrigerator and stove cleaned spotless before morning. When you're done you may sleep on the floor, beside my bed."

He seemed stunned, but dutifully crawled off to begin a task Karin figured would take at least two hours.

As he crawled away, she threw a pillow and a blanket on the floor. Karin drifted off to sleep but awakened hours later when she heard him settling in on the floor. She sprawled out in the bed and went back to sleep.

Karin awoke at 5:00 a.m., took the crop and struck Steven's naked thighs. He struggled to his feet saying, "I thought -"

"Shut up bitch," she yelled. She hit him again. "I know what you thought. You thought last night was a game. WRONG! Assume your position, on your knees, hands behind your head!"

He quickly assumed the position, a look of surprise and fear on his face.

Karin rose from her bed and stood, towering over him. She intended to keep him on his knees a lot. It emphasized her dominance and put him closer to her bottom, feet, and sex; things he would soon learn to love, worship, and cherish above all.

She put a foot to his chest and pushed him toward the door. "I'm going to go back to bed. You will take a shower and shave your cock, balls, and legs. Prepare warm towels for my bath. Return here at 5:45 to lick and massage my feet. At 6:00 you will awaken me and receive further instructions." She returned to her bed as he crawled to the door.

The warm tongue on the sole of her foot stirred her awake. She looked at the clock; it was 5:47. *Is he late or did I just now notice his attentions? No matter, Mistress is always right.* "You're late."

"But I -"

"Shut up! That's extra punishment for lateness and for talking back, five blows each with the leather strap." She watched his shoulders sag. *Poor dear, no matter what he does I'll punish him. It hasn't yet occurred to him that his situation was hopeless. He really thinks that if he tries hard enough he can avoid punishment. It'll never happen. I'll make sure he fails; he'll never live up to my standards. I intended to be an impossible-to-please bitch. But it will be delicious fun to watch him try so hard and fail, to live in fear of my displeasure and punishments.*

Her daydreaming was interrupted by his contrite voice, "Mistress, its 6:00 a.m."

As she arose from the bed she saw him assume his position. *So, men can be trained.*

"Stand up," she ordered. He did, keeping his hands behind his neck. Karin felt his crotch and legs, her soft hands feeling the hair and stubble he'd missed. *Not a bad job, but clearly an amateur one. He'll get better with practice.* She walked to the dresser to retrieve a tool, returning to him and holding it before his eyes.

"Do you know what this is?"

"No, Mistress."

"You should. You gave it to me as a Christmas present a few years ago. It's one of those worthless ideas, a product invented by men for women." It was a hair removal tool, a wretched device that ripped the hairs from a woman's body. She felt his legs and found some places he missed. Karin slowly ran the tool down to that spot. In a slow, cruel and sensuous manner, she used it to remove the offending hairs, taking delight in watching him squirm. *How nice.*

"Does it hurt?"

"Yes, Mistress."

"Did you shave close everywhere? I certainly hope so, because I intend to finish the job with this instrument." He cringed. She felt around his balls and ass hole. "Darling, seems like you missed some places."

Karin ordered him to bend over and spread his legs.

Taking as much time as she could, she finished his hair removal job. She'd expected he'd miss some of those hard-to-get places, where the hair is fine and the flesh is oh-so tender. While she slowly removed the offending hair she scolded him, warning him that if he couldn't do an adequate job with the razor that she'd personally see to it. By the time she finished there were tears in his eyes.

"Stand up!" She felt around his ass and cock. "I expect these areas to be kept clean and smooth at all times. Start using lotion and moisturizer. Keep your ass nice and soft too, a soft tender ass shows my crop and whip better." She pinched his ass. "Bring my black slippers."

He crawled away and quickly returned with her black slippers, the ones with the three inch heels. Karin held out her feet as he slipped them on. The heels added to her commanding presence and made her feel even sexier.

"Lick them clean, and hurry." He bent quickly to the task, running his tongue over the smooth leather tops and heels. "Enough! Go prepare my shower." He didn't crawl away fast enough to escape more blows from her crop.

After he prepared the shower she dismissed him so he could dress for work. He was ordered to return in twenty minutes to towel her dry. When Karin stepped from the shower he was kneeling with warm towels in his outstretched arms.

"You may dry me," she ordered. He began with her feet and worked his way up. It was a luxurious feeling to be pampered so. Karin felt like a Queen, a Goddess. She

leaned against the sink, spreading her legs and exposing her bottom.

"Lick it," she commanded. "Get that tongue in there
and lick my ass like it's the last thing you'll ever taste.
Make love to my ass, worship it."

He went about his task with passion, while Karin
closed her eyes and reveled in the luxury of a male
tongue snaking its way into her crevice. *I hope he really
enjoys this because I know I do, and I expect to have a lot
more of his tongue worship of my lovely bottom.* Karin
enjoyed his efforts for several glorious minutes before
she ordered him to finish drying her off.

When Karin was dry he put the slippers back on her
feet and followed to assist her in dressing. She wanted
him to see her naked, dressing, and undressing. She
wanted him to yearn for her, desire her. Of course he
couldn't have her, at least not on his terms. He could
only have what she gave him and she intended to make
him suffer, grovel and beg for whatever little she would
allow.

As she dressed Karin could see the lust in his eyes.
She teased him unmercifully, making him help her on
with her panties, a particularly sexy pair. She brushed
her sex by his nose so he could smell her fragrance. As
he assisted her with her bra she caressed her full
breasts. Karin knew he wanted to touch them, to kiss,
lick and suck them. Of course he would be denied. As
she pulled on her thigh-high stockings and smoothed
them over her legs she thought he would cum. She made
him crawl back and forth to the closet, fetching pair after
pair of shoes, as she searched for just the right pair of
heels to wear that day. When she finally selected the

perfect pair she made sure he licked them spotlessly clean. *After all, a woman can't go to work with dirty shoes, especially when she has a slave to clean them.* Karin made a mental note to have them cleaned after work also. As she put on her makeup she had him model several pairs of earrings. It amused her to clip them on and make him move his head to see how they looked. The whole dressing experience produced the desired effect. He was turned on by her dressing, humiliated at the shoe cleaning and earring modeling, and sexually frustrated. *I wouldn't be surprised if he scurries to the restroom at his office and jacks off. Hmm, maybe I should invest in a chastity belt to prevent that?*

Before they left for work she turned him over her knee and gave his bottom a good spanking until it was red. With another quick licking of her shoes to insure they were spotless she ordered him to stand and re-leased him from his slave status for the morning. Even so, the drive to work was quiet. He seemed deep in thought, perhaps too scared to speak or question. Perhaps he was concerned about the coming weekend. Karin knew he had reason to be.

Two Months Later

Friday, a glorious weekend of fun, relaxation, and pampering lay ahead of Karin. Not so for her poor hus-band and slave, who faced a weekend of servitude, humiliation, pain, and degradation. In only a few short weeks Karin molded her husband into the perfect sub-missive, personal slave and 'maid.'

Within minutes Steven stood before her, naked and ready for inspection, save for the wide leather collar around his neck. In his mouth he held a chain leash. His hands were clasped behind his neck, his feet spread apart; just as he had been trained.

Karin picked up the crop and playfully poked and prodded his cock and balls. When his eyes glanced down she quickly slapped his thigh with the crop. "Keep those eyes straight ahead!"

He winced at the blow but dutifully followed her command.

Karin ordered him to turn around and bend over at the waist, exposing his tender ass. She continued tormenting his cock and balls, this time from the rear, poking around his ass hole, and occasionally slapping his ass with the crop. She reached forward and felt his balls and legs. His shaving skills were improving but she noted a few deficiencies. *Another session with my tool is in order. Maybe I'll use it on his underarms.*

Karin's long nails raked his cock and balls. "What happens to naughty little French maids?"

"They get fucked in the ass, Mistress," he mumbled with the leash in his mouth.

"And do you deserve a fucking?"

"If it pleases my Mistress."

My pleasure. Yes, I'll have my pleasure this weekend. Karin clapped her hands once and he quickly turned and knelt before her, leaning forward to offer the leash in his mouth. His hands were still clasped behind his neck, the result of training, discipline and more than a few beatings. She took the leash and snapped it on his collar.

Karin snapped her fingers and pointed to her feet. She had had not changed out of her work clothes and still wore her black business pumps, which needed cleaning. He immediately put his tongue to work, licking away the dust and dirt which should never be found on the high heels of the superior woman. While he licked her shoes clean she picked up a notebook to read him the offenses he'd committed during the week. For these he would face a weekend of pain, submission, service, and humiliation.

"You failed to properly fold and hang up the towels. You forgot to dust above the refrigerator. You failed to show the proper respect to my friend Sandra. You were five minutes late picking me up on Tuesday." The list went on, the punishments adding up. He would always fail at something. She was impossible to please, although that didn't mean he should ever stop trying. As she read she lifted her feet so he could suck the heels clean. Finally satisfied that her shoes were properly serviced, she clapped her hands twice and stood up.

Steven quickly assumed a position on his hands and knees, at her feet.

With a tug on his leash she led him toward the bedroom. As her heels clicked down the hallway he crawled behind, her faithful, obedient pet.

Satin, lace, silk, nylon and spandex, for a woman these can be items of sensuous luxury, bringing much pleasure. Karin used these same items on her slave, to inflict pain, humiliation and degradation. They were very effective tools, when used in the proper manner, for training, disciplining and subjugating males who have not yet learned to worship and serve women. Once in the bedroom she ordered him to stand. It was time to dress him for an evening's fun.

The first item was a black corset. Karin purchased one that was very feminine, yet hideously restrictive. It was a size too small, on purpose, and heavily boned. Her primary goal was to create discomfort and to humiliate, but it also gave him a pleasing feminine shape and correct posture. It was almost as good as bondage, as it greatly restricted his movements. Even when kneeling, crawling or sitting it demanded a very correct, and uncomfortable, posture. Of course it was uncomfortable, she meant it to be. Whenever he wore it he suffered for her pleasure - and she enjoyed that.

Using a paddle on his bare ass, and ordering him to, "Suck it in, suck it in," she finally got it fastened. He also wore other foundation garments to amuse her. Sometimes she put him in a tight, long legged and boned panty girdle. This was useful when she plugged his ass; the tight garment was an excellent way to keep those objects firmly in place. Other times he wore an open panty girdle so she could view, and punish, his cock and balls. She also bought him garter belts and waist cinchers. He was going to be made to suffer in every wretched piece of female undergarment she could find or devise. Tonight though, it was the corset.

Stockings were next. Karin debated; sheer or fishnet? She decided on a pair of black, seamed, fishnet stockings, and these were fastened to the garters on his corset. A few hours of a foot clad in a fishnet stocking in a spike heel can be very uncomfortable, even painful. By the end of the evening Steven would beg to relieve himself of this torment. Crawling to Karin on his hands and knees would be a treat for him, one she would probably deny.

Next were the shoes. Karin's feet were smaller than his, but in stockings, and with enough pushing and pinching he could wear them. Perfect! Breaking in a new pair of shoes, especially four or five inch stiletto heels, can be a pain, literally. That's the beauty in having one's own maid, someone to break in your shoes. This evening Karin chose a pair of black patent, sling back, five inch spike heels. These definitely needed breaking in. After some motivation with her riding crop he finally got them on.

"Too tight?" she mocked.

"Yes, Mistress," he replied.

Well, bad for him, good for me, his pain, my pleasure. Karin ordered him to walk around the room, following as he tottered around on the tall, spindly heels. She used her crop to emphasize comments and criticisms on his performance. "I want a dainty, sexy maid; take smaller steps, and put more hip movement into it." He got better with practice

Karin had actually designed a sexy black and white maid's uniform for him, but decided against it for to-night. She intended that uniform for when he would serve and entertain her girlfriends, something he had yet to experience. No, for tonight a simple white lace apron would do. It was a long sheer apron that had shoulder straps, went to his knees and tied behind the waist in a big bow; very feminine, but not very practical. His cock and balls were clearly visible beneath the diaphanous fabric.

She couldn't help but notice how his cock had swollen and begun to drip that disgusting ooze. The erotic clothes, the pain, the humiliation all had a strong effect on him. Karin lifted up the apron to expose his manhood, wiped his cum off with her finger and held it to his lips. He opened his mouth, no longer having to be told, and sucked and licked her cum-soaked finger clean.

Karin strictly controlled his sexual releases. Except for basic biological and hygiene functions he was not allowed to touch himself except at her direction. She supervised his masturbation and decided whether or not he would ejaculate. Unauthorized releases were met with severe punishment and discipline. She deliberately dressed in very sexy clothes as this greatly excited him, and teased his cock, nipples and ass relentlessly, warning him not to come and punishing him when he failed to obey. He had still not learned control. In all cases he was required to lick up and swallow his messes. Karin made him wear a condom so she could be sure to get it all. She enjoyed feeding it to him with a small silver spoon, putting it on a dildo and having him suck it off, or smearing it on a pair of wicked spike heels and watching him use his tongue to shine her shoes with it. She was becoming very creative, and cruel, but still he obeyed.

"If you serve me well this weekend I may allow you to come," she teased.

"Thank you, Mistress."

There was still more dressing to do. Karin added black elbow-length gloves. Although maids didn't usually wear such, they looked good with his black corset, stockings and heels.

Jewelry was next. Thorough shopping expeditions to boutiques, thrift shops and bargain counters provided choice pieces. Karin searched exclusively for items that were painful, uncomfortable and humiliating. Tonight she selected a pair of earrings that were very long, heavy and, most important, very uncomfortable. She clipped them on his ears and noted with satisfaction how they hung heavily almost to his shoulders, and instructed him to move his head around so she could see how they moved. They swung heavily and noisily, pulling at his ear lobes. She'd used pliers on all his earrings to adjust them for a tight and painful fit. If they didn't hurt now; in a few hours they would.

Finally she pinched his nipples until they were hard and erect. When she had them just right Karin attached his nipple clamps. Throughout the evening she would tighten and loosen them. He was very susceptible to nipple torments and would not be able to control his passion, so she added a condom so as not to miss anything.

Karin finally stood back to admire her work. What a slut he was! She felt sure he was in for a very uncomfortable evening.

She ordered him to model for her and he did quarter turns, executing a small bob curtsey at each new position. "Excellent," she beamed. "You've become quite the feminized, submissive slut in the last few weeks. You need a new name, Steven won't do; and I can't always call you slave, or bitch. Suzette! Yes, from now on you'll be Suzette. Say it, say your new name."

"I'm Sissy Maid Suzette."

Karin sat in a chair and lit a cigarette. "Say it again, keep turning and keep saying your new name."

Steven, now Suzette's, eyes filled with shame and the head dropped a bit in defeat. But s/he turned - and bobbed - and spoke: "I'm Sissy Maid Suzette, I'm Sissy Maid Suzette, I'm Sissy Maid Suzette."

Karin shook her head in amazement, *Perfect, absolutely perfect.*

Three

$\mathcal{K}$arin began enlisting her cadre of wicked friends and acquaintances to assist with Suzette's transformation. Trudi Schwarz became Suzette's aerobics instructor and dance teacher. Suzette had regular dance and exercise sessions with Trudi and many of these were videotaped for Karin's amusement.

Trudi was originally from Germany, where she worked as an exotic dancer in some of the better erotic sex clubs in Hamburg. Now, in the United States, she owned and operated a small chain of women's exercise salons cashing in on the latest "pole dancing" exercise craze. Trudi didn't mind taking money from bored, cellulite conscious housewives in return for showing them how to "work it" on the pole. These female clientele with their fat checkbooks and husband's credit cards were an improvement over those perverse and sleazy types with their wrinkled and greasy one-dollar bills. There had never been enough of the really big spenders to offset those losers looking for a cheap thrill. Some say that she was known to moonlight in some of the more extreme and perverse of erotic Euro offerings. At a finely toned, yet curvy five feet ten, with her blonde hair slicked back, one didn't need much imagination to picture her in leather and latex and wielding a crop. Her latent cruel streak was certainly evident in her training of Suzette, or Karin would not have hired her.

It was Karin's plan to diet and exercise her submissive Suzette down to a pleasing feminine shape, finishing off the look with corset training, foundation wear and, if necessary, perhaps even hormones. For now, however, it was a strict regimen of diet, dance and exercise. And with Trudi, strict was strict.

Trudi typically arrived in the early afternoon, after Suzette finished with Karin's morning domestic needs and completed the usual list of chores for that day. Suzette would be attired in whatever costume was required for the day's lesson: a cute little spandex leotard for aerobic work or a slutty, stripper, pole dance outfit for 'dance class.'

Today's session was erotic dance. Karin had designs of making an erotic dancer out of Suzette, someone to entertain Karin's friends and lovers. *There's nothing like a bit of erotic dance to get a man all hot, sexy and hard* mused Karin. She imagined the shame and embarrassment that would be felt by Suzette as she strutted and pranced in her little dance outfit while Karin and her boyfriend snuggled on the couch. Karin's husband, now her slave and maid, would get her lover aroused and then watch as he and Karin walked arm-in-arm to the bedroom. Suzette would entertain them, clean up after them, and then change into her maid's outfit to serve them later. *A slut to turn them on and a maid to clean up after them, that's how a good husband serves his wife's lovers* thought Karin.

The costume that Karin selected that morning was a new one. It had a matching red top and bottom, both very skimpy and dripping with fringe. By the end of the day Trudi would have that fringe shaking in the most seductive manner. Black, thigh-high fishnets and long red gloves added to the erotic nature of the outfit. Of course Suzette had on her special 'dance wig', a long and heavy mane of dirty blonde tresses that she would swing and shake. All dance sessions were performed in six-inch heels, and today's footwear sported a clear heel with a two inch platform and red beaded accents to complement the red top and bottom. Trashy, dangly earrings and a wrist full of sparkly faux diamond bracelets completed the accessories. Suzette's make up was extreme, as befitted a partially clothed erotic dancer.

Suzette wore a light robe over her outfit and answered the door exactly at 1:00 when Trudi, ever the precise and methodical German, breezed through the door, ignoring the hapless Suzette. The dance and exercise sessions were one of the few times that Karin's 'stoop low so you are never taller than any woman' rule was not enforced. It was, after all, dance and they were working on posture. Still, even in her six-inch heels Suzette was shorter than Trudi, who usually wore high-heeled boots and loomed over the hapless Suzette.

Trudi reached into a nearby umbrella stand and retrieved a thin rattan cane. She walked to Suzette and delivered a blow to Suzette's ass, the flimsy robe offering no protection against the vicious reed.

"Remove the robe. Schnell!" demanded Trudi, threatening another blow with the cane.

Suzette quickly let the robe fall from her shoulders and hung it on a nearby hook. *Schnell, fast* she thought resignedly. *Sure, I'm learning German words and phrases but this is a lousy way to become bilingual.*

With no further discussion Trudi turned on her heel and walked to the basement, Suzette precariously mincing behind. Karin was turning part of the basement into a cozy night club environment that would accommodate several couples - and one cute barmaid, cocktail waitress and erotic dancer. Trudi's friends built a small dance stage complete with a pole and mirrored back walls. There was a small wooden dance floor in front of the stage. Karin was having great fun decorating and selecting various carpets, love seats and small tables. The seating arrangement could easily be turned to face the large, flat panel TV on the rear wall. Karin had plans of hosting football parties and other such sporting events. She was even designing a sexy little cheerleader outfit for Suzette. At half time Suzette could get up on her stage and dance for Karin's guests and friends, a little half-time entertainment. Then it would be back to serving drinks and snacks and giving foot rubs and pedicures to the women. And for the men...well...Karin was working on that one as well; what better way to celebrate when your team scores but to 'score' yourself!

Trudi relaxed in one of the chairs and idly tapped the cane against her leg. "Let me see your walk. Have you been practicing?"

"Yes Miss Trudi." Suzette walked across the dance floor, trying to remember all the instructions from the last lesson and execute her drill flawlessly.

Trudi watched in steely silence, her gray-green eyes taking in every detail of Suzette's performance. She continued to watch as Suzette made five trips up and back across the small wooden dance floor. The only sounds were the clicking of Suzette's stiletto heels on the wooden dance floor, punctuated by the occasional 'whap' of the cane as Trudi idly slapped it against her boot.

Finally, Trudi had seen enough and rose to confront Suzette. "Liebchen, we went over this already. It's supposed to be erotic, sensual, seductive. You walk like you are delivering the morning milk or carrying groceries." Trudi lashed out with the cane, leaving a thin, red welt at the top of Suzette's thighs, just below her bottom.

Suzette stood still, hands at her sides, trying to concentrate on Trudi's instructions. She had to get this right because pissing off this Euro-bitch would unleash a Teutonic tirade of Wagnerian proportions.

Trudi went to the back of the dance floor and turned to face Suzette. "Watch me Liebchen." Trudi slowly walked forward. She prowled, like a dangerous jungle cat. Her hips rolled, her eyes locked on Suzette's.

Suzette was mesmerized by Trudi's sensual gait and seductive gaze.

"Remember Liebchen, walk slowly, step out, forward with one foot and slowly drag the rear foot forward, step-drag, step-drag."

"Yes, Miss Trudi," gasped Suzette. For a second Suzette had a fleeting memory of a gentlemen's club, drinking with the guys, slipping dollar bills into the stockings of dancers. It all seemed so long ago, so foreign now.

Trudi stopped before Suzette and looked down at her. "As a maid, you should avoid eye contact. But as a dancer you need to look at your audience, get them involved, bring them into your dance. Use your arms and hands to draw them close to you." Trudi executed 'come hither' snake-like movements with her arms.

Suzette was beginning to understand, but could she

really do this? Could she really be the seductive little tramp to excite Mistress Karin and her lover while they sat on the couch and enjoyed the show?

"As you walk, exaggerate your hip movements," said Trudi. She walked and rolled her hips ,and then stopped to face Suzette. She could see the maid was slightly flushed and breathing a little faster. Trudi smiled, *Yes I still 'have it' if I can make a little, feminized, submissive, sissy maid pant with desire. Now if I can only teach this little slut to do that to Mistress Karin's lovers then I will have earned my money.*

"Try again," said Trudi. "Remember, posture, be confident, you are sexy, you are desirable, bring the audience into your dance." Trudi turned and went to the console at the side of the sofa, dimmed the lights and turned on the music. "Do it," she commanded. "Walk for me, make me hot."

Trudi's dominant presence, sexy demonstration and dirty talk had excited Suzette, and she backed up to the edge of the dance floor to begin her sexy walk. It was better this time, with the lights low and the music.

"Again!" ordered Trudi.

Suzette spent the next twenty minutes walking back and forth. Trudi made comments and corrections, but the sexy parade never stopped. After twenty minutes Suzette's legs and calves ached from the postured movement.

Finally Trudi reached over, shut off the music and turned up the lights. She smiled; Karin was going to be pleased. "Much better, much better, now we do floor work."

Four

As soon as the doorbell rang she quickly stopped what she was doing and rushed to the door. Suzette would be punished for tardiness if a guest had to ring twice. Mistress Karin did not like for her guests or visitors to be kept waiting.

Unfortunately, rushing to the door was not so easy. The maid's day uniform required the wearing of five inch stiletto heels and Suzette had been rigorously trained to take small, dainty, heel-toe steps. Complicating the matter was the visitor's impatience, after a short pause following the first ring the visitor rang two more times in quick succession. Though punishment was now assured, Suzette quickened her pace, knowing a fourth ring would make it worse. The quicker pace on the tottering heels drove the tightly-strapped anal plug deeper into her ass with each mincing step.

Suzette reached the door before the fourth ring and took a quick second to straighten her maid's dress and apron before opening the door. She recognized Mistress Karin's visitor as Sheila Remington. Suzette curtsied daintily and greeted the visitor.

"Good morning Ms. Remington."

Sheila Remington was an attractive woman in her mid-40s, with a woman's voluptuous curves. Her auburn hair was elegantly coiffed and her makeup impeccably applied. She wore a stylish, skirted suit that was well fitted for her figure. Expensive pumps with four inch heels adorned her feet. She slowly removed her kid leather gloves and eyed the maid before her.

Suzette was of average build and at five-foot seven in five inch heels should have towered over Mistress Remington. But Suzette had been trained, even when wearing the highest of heels, to crouch and stoop so as to be shorter than the ladies she served. Mistress Remington gazed down at the frilly, feminine thing before her.

Suzette wore a knee-length black satin maid's dress. White petticoats filled it out and nicely accented the white lace apron and lace accents on the dress. Wrist-length lace gloves, a satin neck choker and a white lace maid's cap completed the outfit. Her legs were encased in black seamed stockings and her feet crammed into black patent stiletto heels with pointed toes. She remained silent, crouching, hands folded demurely in front, awaiting the next command.

Mistress Remington circled the maid, her stylish pumps clicking on the foyer tile floor. She touched the maid's waist. "I see your Mistress has corseted you. Do you like it?"

"Yes, Miss Remington," said Suzette.

Sheila stepped in front of the maid and, with an elegantly manicured nail, lifted the maid's chin. "Why

Suzette, you're wearing makeup!"

Suzette's lips were a crimson red and the eyes highlighted with blue eye shadow and extremely long false eyelashes. A short black wig and long dangling earrings completed maid's look.

"Yes, Suzette, you're turning into quite the lovely little thing. I bet Karin's male guests can't keep their hands off you." Sheila smiled at the pained look that came over the maid's face. "Run along and put my things away."

Suzette took the gloves, hat, and coat of Mistress Remington and teetered off to put them away. As she walked away Sheila slipped her hand under the maid's dress and pinched her ass. "Remember dear, small, dainty steps." Sheila laughed as she walked into the living room.

Karin Calloway rose from her chair to greet her guest as Sheila entered the room. "Sheila, you look stunning! Are you ready for some shopping?"

"Karin dear, of course, and you also look wonderful. And your shoes! Are those new Manolos?"

The two women lightly embraced then stepped back. Karin Calloway extended her right foot to display a stylish sling-back pump with a stiletto heel. "Yes, these are new. Aren't they divine?"

"Oh yes," replied Sheila. "I must look for some today."

The women seated themselves on the couch in Karin's tastefully decorated living room. Karin was also in her mid-forties, tall, and still with a decent figure. Her medium length red hair framed an oval face with features that could, at times, be stern and taciturn. But her expertly applied makeup and tasteful jewelry softened those features and gave her an attractive, almost aristocratic air. She wore a well fitted Chanel suit that flattered her long legs, ending in the stiletto heels. The overall effect would surely catch the eye of many, men and women alike, when she entered a room.

"Would you like some wine?" asked Karin.

"Yes, that would be lovely, thank you," replied Sheila.

Karin picked up a small crystal bell from the table and gave it a couple of quick rings. The two women looked at each other and exchanged wicked smiles. A few seconds later Suzette entered the room, approached with the required short, dainty steps, and stopped, executing a deep curtsey before the two women. "Suzette, we'd like some white wine before we go shopping and bring me a cigarette."

Suzette quickly retrieved the cigarette holder from the wooden box on the table, inserted a dark, European cigarillo and handed Karin the cigarette holder, bending over deeply at the waist to expose her ass. Sheila nodded approvingly at the submissive display.

Karin took the cigarette holder from her maid and waited while the Suzette proffered a light. Suzette remained bent over while Karin lit her cigarette and then exhaled a stream of smoke into Suzette's face. "Perhaps our guest would also like a cigarette," said Karin. Suzette turned to face Mistress Remington who had already removed her own cigarette holder from her purse. The cigarette lighting procedure was repeated for Mistress Remington and then Suzette was dismissed to fetch the wine. The women laughed.

"Karin, you've done a wonderful job. He's becoming extremely obedient, docile and feminine."

"Yes," replied Karin, "everything a proper husband should be."

After Suzette served the wine Karin said, "You may dust in here while we talk."

Suzette curtsied and returned with the feather duster. In preparation for Mistress Remington's visit Suzette had cleaned and dusted the room the night before and again that morning. She knew that the room didn't need any cleaning. *The damned room is spotless! I'm just dusting to entertain the ladies.* With the duster in her right hand and her left hand placed sexily on her left hip, Suzette proceeded to mince around the room with short dainty steps. When dusting low objects she made it a point to bend low, at the waist, to show the frilly panties that Karin made her wear. The two women continued to sit on the sofa, drink their wine and make small talk. They hardly seemed to pay attention to Suzette's chores. But Suzette knew that the slightest dereliction in her duties would be noticed and would earn her immediate punishment.

"I noticed that Suzette was wearing makeup, that's rather new, isn't it?" asked Sheila.

"Yes," replied Karin, "it's something we just started a few days ago. And it hasn't been easy."

"Really?"

"Oh you should have seen it," explained Karin,

"Suzette threw such a little hissy fit."

Karin snapped her fingers. "Suzette!"

Suzette immediately assumed her position. "Turn around and show Sheila your ass," ordered Karin.

Suzette turned and bent at the waist. She lifted her maid's dress and petticoats and pulled down the pretty panties to reveal an ass covered with purple welts.

"Your crop?" asked Sheila.

"Yes, after an extended session with the crop, Suzette became more amenable to the idea of make-up, didn't you dear?"

"Yes, Mistress," replied Suzette.

"Come closer," ordered Mistress Remington.

Suzette backed up, tottering precariously on her heels.

Sheila used one long and exquisite fingernail and slowly traced a line over one of the welts. Suzette flinched, the area was quite tender. Karin picked up the ever-present crop from the table, quickly and expertly striking a blow directly over one of the welts.

"Don't fidget!" barked Karin. "My guest wants to examine you."

Sheila continued her wicked examination of Suzette's ass. "You know I had to ring three times today."

"Yes, I'm sorry about that," replied Karin. "Of course you may punish her for that."

"Thank you, I'd enjoy that. I think I'd like to redden that little ass with a paddle. Perhaps Suzette can fetch the wooden paddle?"

Karin clapped her hands. Suzette stood up, straightened her dress, and curtsied to the women on the way to her errand.

"Karin, darling, she's an absolute jewel! You've done a wonderful job."

"Well," replied Karin, "some parts of the training have been easier than others. Strict discipline and punishment had to be used. A lot of submissive men like that, up to a point. Taking them past that point, to the unknown and unfamiliar is where we really break them and begin to control them completely. And yet... Suzette was easier than most; as a husband he worshipped and was devoted to me. So it was really only a matter of reinforcing those submissive tendencies and then feminizing him into Suzette the maid."

"But don't you miss men?"

Karin laughed. "Darling, I intend having lovers whenever I want them, but always on my terms. I've already picked out the first one. And of course when they come to call Suzette will greet them and wait on them. She'll prepare me for my dates, bathe me, do my feet, and shine my shoes. It will torment and humiliate her so. But she knows it will please me so she'll accept it, not that the little bitch really has any choice in the matter. Of course many of my lovers will want oral sex, but I simply abhor the idea of taking a man's cock into my mouth. But men do seem to like it don't they? I've considered relegating those duties to Suzette."

"You'd have your husband suck your lover's cock!"

"Suzette, my maid, would perform those services for my lovers. I don't imagine they really care who it is sucking them off as long as they get to shoot their load into the pert, soft mouth of some slut. I'd dress Suzette in a short, tight skirt and fuck-me pumps so my dates could get sucked off by a real slut. I've had her practice on a dildo. I do want her to be proficient at it. Oh, here's our little slut now, with the paddle."

Suzette returned with the paddle, stood in front of the two women and curtsied.

"Miss Remington, I apologize for my poor performance in answering the door today and beg you to administer discipline with this paddle." Suzette bowed low, and extended the long wooden paddle to Sheila.

"Thank you Suzette, depending on how well you accept my beating I may accept your apology." Sheila took the paddle. "How many strokes do you recommend?" she asked Suzette.

"Perhaps six would be sufficient, Miss Remington?" Suzette's voice was halting, with a trace of fear and trepidation.

"No my dear. I shall deliver twelve of the best, and expect you to earnestly beg for more when I'm done." She and Karin exchanged wicked smiles and laughed.

"Thank you, Miss Remington." Suzette's reply was resigned and fearful. *Twelve with the wooden paddle across my crop-marked ass is going to hurt. And Mistress Remington is expecting me to beg, and beg sincerely, for more. Shit!*

"You marked her up with your crop Karin, I'm

afraid the paddle is only going to make things worse."

Karin idly shrugged her shoulders in a 'so what' gesture. *If they do what they're told they won't get beaten, well, most of the time.*

Sheila rose from the sofa and led Suzette to the center of the living room. Suzette bent over, pulled down her panties and held up her dress and petticoats, exposing her ass. Sheila raked her nails over the welts and Suzette flinched. Sheila smiled and cooed, "So tender, poor baby."

The first blow landed on the right ass cheek directly over the welts from Karin's crop. The second blow landed in exactly the same place, as did the third. Suzette's knees were shaking. *Not fair, not fair!* Suzette moaned to herself, *they're supposed to distribute the blows, move them around.*

Sheila stopped to rake her nails over the reddening ass and purple welts before delivering a fourth blow to the same place.

Suzette's ass was on fire, her knees shaking uncontrollably. She wanted to use her hands to protect her ass, but to do that was to invite a worse and longer punishment.

Sheila continued her assault, placing the remaining blows in different places, but always over the red crop welts. The sixth blow landed, mercifully enough, lower, on the back of the right thigh. Sheila walked in front of Suzette and held the paddle to Suzette's face. Suzette kissed the paddle, "Thank you Miss Remington."

Sheila delivered the last six blows, alternating them between the left and right ass cheeks.

When finished, she walked in front of Suzette and lifted her chin with the paddle. Tears were streaming down Suzette's face. Sheila smiled, "Well?"

"Thank you, Miss Remington," stammered Suzette between sobs, "May I please have six more?"

Sheila reached around and raked her nails across Suzette's sore and reddened ass. "SIX!" Sheila yelled. "You think I should waste my time with another measly six!?!" Sheila brutally pinched Suzette's ass.

"Please, oh please Mistress, another seven... please?"

"Bitch!" yelled Sheila and slapped Suzette's face. Karin nodded approvingly.

Suzette was beside herself. "Please Mistress, another ten, please I beg you."

Sheila stood silently before Suzette, idly and menacingly slapping the paddle against her thigh.

Resignedly, Suzette, her voice near breaking, pleaded, "Please, Mistress, please, another twelve, I beg you, please." She was near panic and desperate at the thought of begging for twelve more, but to refuse, to refuse, that would only invite something worse. Suzette was going to have to dig down and find a way to get through it.

"Yes", nodded Sheila, "yes, I believe you do beg me. Stay bitch!"

Suzette remained bent, holding up her dress and petticoats. Her back and legs hurt from holding the position, her ass was a sea of pain, and yet there was more to come. She was in despair. She could hear the women behind her talking in hushed tones and laughing. Then she heard a ripping sound.

Sheila walked in front of Suzette and showed her two pieces of duct tape, each piece about two inches by six inches. Smiling, Sheila walked behind Suzette and roughly applied a piece of tape to each tender, swollen and red buttock.

The next twelve blows with the dreaded wooden paddle were applied evenly, six to each piece of tape. After the last blow Suzette was sobbing and shaking, but she'd held her position.

Sheila once again appeared in front of Suzette and held the paddle before Suzette's trembling lips. Through her tears Suzette kissed the paddle. "Thank you, Mistress."

Sheila laughed. "I accept your apology, Suzette, and now we must remove the tape."

Suzette felt hands probing her bruised and battered ass and sharp fingernails digging in the tender flesh around the tape. Mistress Remington finally got an edge of the tape loose and started to s-l-o-w-l-y pull it off.

"You may cry and wail and beg me to stop, Suzette. In fact it would please me to hear you do so." Sheila continued to slowly remove the tape, using her free hand and her elegant fingernails to scratch and pinch the bruised and raw flesh.

"No! Stop! Please stop, no, no, please stop," wailed Suzette. After the first piece of tape was removed Sheila gave the exposed flesh a stinging slap with her hand. Suzette shuddered. The entire process was repeated on the other ass cheek, the tape slowly removed and the exposed flesh violated.

Finally finished administering the punishment,

Sheila Remington returned to the couch. "I need a cigarette."

Karin clapped her hands. "Suzette, bring us more wine and a cigarette!"

Suzette stood up, straightened her dress, petticoats and apron, put cigarettes in ladies holders, and then lit the cigarettes. She curtsied, rather clumsily, and left to fetch the wine.

"Well done," Karin said.

"Yes," replied Sheila, "she won't be able to sit down tomorrow, but she took it well enough."

When the women finished their wine and cigarettes they stood and prepared to leave. Karin rang the bell to summon Suzette.

Suzette entered and curtsied, crouching so she was shorter than the dominant and superior females who stood before her. Her eyes were red from crying.

"We're leaving," Karin said, "get our things."

Suzette curtsied and left to get the women's coats, hats, gloves and purses. The two women walked into the foyer where Suzette was waiting. As Suzette assisted them with their coats Karin snapped her fingers and pointed to her feet. While the women pulled on their kid leather gloves, Suzette knelt to give their shoes a final cleaning with her tongue.

The two women made small talk while Suzette lavishly tongued their fashionable pumps clean. Finally satisfied, Karin kicked Suzette away. "Up!" she ordered.

Suzette rose to her submissive crouch.

"We're going shopping, you have your list of chores," said Karin. "Oh, be sure to practice your dancing. I'm having a party this weekend and I expect my guests to be suitably entertained. I want a lot of hot, slutty moves. Trudi says you're coming along nicely so we're expecting quite a show." Both women turned on the heels of their elegant footwear and walked out.

Suzette slowly walked to the kitchen to get the list of chores she would perform.

Five

Karin used a small piece of toast to wipe up the egg yolk on her breakfast plate. Without looking, she held out the morsel of food and felt it gently removed from her hand. She didn't have to see the scene unfold to know what happened. These small offerings had become valued treats for Suzette.

On some mornings Karin snapped her fingers and pointed to the floor. Suzette immediately knelt beside her Mistress, hoping that her bland diet might be augmented by those few precious scraps of 'real' food. Since her submission her diet had been meager at best. The morning gruel, often flavored with cigarette ashes, Mistress's 'nectar' or spit was supplanted by a wretched concoction called *Prison Loaf*. Karin discovered the loaf during a web search and it now formed the basis of Suzette's second meal of the day. The loaf was a mixture of grated carrots, wheat bread, artificial cheese, spinach, beans, and raisins – among other items. It was unappetizing, and purposely meant to be. That's why Suzette would literally sit and beg for table scraps.

Karin idly turned the business pages and sipped her coffee. "How long since you've been to the office?"

"Maybe two months, Mistress?" He phrased it as a question, he truly didn't know.

She didn't press the issue, content with his answer. It was what she wanted – his isolation from the world at large – total focus and dependence on her. He was kept busy all day with chores, tasks, dance lessons, aerobic workouts in cute pink leotards. He was denied computer and television access, she'd locked those out. Newspapers were forbidden to him, but he was allowed women's magazines: *Vogue, Good Housekeeping,* and *Glamour.*

"Three months," she said. "It's been three months since you had your –'breakdown' – and had to take time off from work. But I've been able to fill in nicely for you; after all, Daddy did leave the company to me."

"Yes, Mistress, but I thought –"

"Wrong! You thought wrong, and that's why I'm doing the thinking now. You thought that the executive with the perfect wife was the ideal. And I agree with you." She waited, wondering if that statement meant he would think they were going back to the old way; he as the CEO and she as the trophy wife. A slight smile crossed her lips as she watched his eyes light up with that hoped-for realization. She'd grown to love these moments, watching as he rose to the bait and savoring his utter desolation when she pulled out the rug and crushed his hopes. *If only his hopes were some kind of living, organic thing that I could crush with my stiletto, feel the spike heel puncture it, watch the life force slowly drain away.*

"One of the girls from the office will be coming by today." She looked him in the eyes; she wanted to remember this moment – and his reaction. "They'll be bringing papers for you to sign, your resignation."

He started to talk, even though he knew he didn't have permission. When Karin held up her hand he quickly shut his mouth.

"You will resign from your position as CEO. You will sign over all of your shares and interests in the company to me. Furthermore, you will sign over all other assets, financial and material, to me." The shock on his face, the fear, it was priceless. "You will sign a general power of attorney giving me complete control over you.

"Yes, we are going to have the perfect corporate marriage. I'm going to be the powerful, high-priced executive. And you, you my little slut, will be the trophy wife, or, in your case, the trophy sissy maid husband. As the executive I'll have trophy lovers, and you will serve them as you do me."

His shoulders fell and his chin dropped to his chest. Karin was surprised at how easily he yielded his manhood to her. She'd now taken everything, reduced him to a servant in her house. "You will sign all the papers put before you."

He meekly nodded, "Yes, Mistress."

She held out a piece of bacon and watched as his eyes lit up and he gently took it between his lips. *I destroy his career, his marriage; take his freedom and his manhood, and a scrap of bacon makes it all better.*

Karin visualized her basement project: the cage, computer, restraints and accessories. Her experiments with operant conditioning and behavior modification worked with Steven; maybe she was on to something.

She rose from the table and walked to the foyer, her husband crawling obediently at her side. "You have your list of chores. And spend thirty minutes practicing walking with the book on your head. Wear your five inch heels; work on that posture and taking the short and dainty steps. There will be times when you won't be crouching and short so you're looking up to women. I may want to pimp you out as a tranny, fetish runway model." She laughed at the thought; Steven, now Suzette, in stilettos, strutting the catwalk and shaking his submissive ass to the gathered throng.

"Be sure to sign all the papers this afternoon. I want this over, behind us, so we can move on. There's no going back." She looked down to see her husband on his knees, planting loving kisses on the toes of her stylish high heels. *No arguments, he simply accepts his situation...amazing. What started out as sex games, a little B & D...* "You'll still be my husband; you'll still keep your cock and balls, although that cock will seldom be out of chastity. And when it is, I can guarantee you won't enjoy it and you'll beg to lock it up. I don't want you to ever forget what you were...or how far you've fallen."

She reached down and patted him on the head. "This really is best, for both of us."

His eyes met hers; he nodded his agreement and returned his lips to her shoes.

Karin arrived at the office, her office, the seat of her new empire, in good spirits. She felt free, even though she was still – technically – married.

Laurel, her secretary, greeted her with coffee and the preliminary financials for the newest corporate venture. "You have a meeting with Acquisitions at ten-thirty and a presentation from Product Development at two." With the grace of a relay baton hand-off Laurel exchanged the coffee in her hand with Karin's purse. "I watched him, oh 'her' – sorry – on the monitor. She cleaned up in the kitchen and went to change for her aerobics."

"Thank you, I have some papers for you to take to my house today." Karin settled into her leather chair and held the coffee cup with two hands. *Life is good.* "Take Sharon with you, she's a Notary isn't she? Make sure my little slut signs them all, you witness and Sharon can notarize."

"Yes, Ms. Calloway." Laurel turned to hang up Karin's coat. "Do you think we might be able to – I mean if it's OK with you – maybe we could –

"You want a play date with my sissy maid." Karin sipped her coffee and placed the cup on her desk. Certainly Laurel was competent and efficient, but had Steven hired her for her physical attributes, some latent submissive tendencies he possessed? At five-ten, and in her four inch heels, Laurel would have towered over Steven. Her blonde hair and blue-eyed beauty would have enthralled any man. "Like what you've been seeing on our office webcams?"

"It's awesome."

Karin chuckled. Laurel was a good fifteen years

younger than her so 'awesome' was probably high praise in that age group lexicon. "He knows that we've been watching him from the office, but he's never been put on real-time, personal display. It might be good for him. And for you and Sharon to show up, his former secretary and Chief of Administration, think how humiliating that will be. Yes, have a good time, put him through his paces as it were. Did he ever forget Secretary's Day?"

"We call it Administrative Professional's Day, but yea, we'd have to remind him and then he'd just tell us to order ourselves some flowers."

Asshole. Karin shook her head. *He probably had them order the flowers for our anniversaries and even shop for the gifts. Well now the flimsy lingerie would still be bought, but worn by the true slut of the house.* She smiled at Laurel, *might as well get them trained right.* "Have a good time; it's your chance for a little revenge. But I want pictures and video, and I want him to know you're taking them and why."

"Yes Ms. Calloway, we'll take good care of him – uh- if you know what I mean. And he never, I mean Steven –

"Suzette."

"Yes, Suzette, she never came on to me or any-thing, tried anything sexual. Maybe he wasn't always the most considerate boss, but –

"Laurel, trust me, I understand. If he did want to get into your panties...it's because he wanted to wear them." Karin saw something in the young secretary's eyes. "What?"

"Oh, it's just that last year...I had this new pair of

heels; I saved for three paydays and had them in my desk drawer and then one morning – they were gone."

Both women shared a knowing moment and then turned their attention to the monitor where Suzette, resplendent in a pink leotard, was bouncing to her workout video.

"Payback time," Karin said.

Laurel smiled at the flouncing sissy maid on the screen, "Payback time."

Suzette put away her workout DVD and went to shower and change her clothes. She knew that every room was equipped with cameras and that Karin, and possibly others, were able to monitor her every move. Under Karin's regime even the shower ritual was feminized; shaving of all body hair, washing with scented soaps, exfoliating and moisturizing. Suzette wrapped a towel around her middle, tucking it in at her bosom. A second towel went around her head, turban style, while she carefully plucked and tweezed her eyebrows into an arch. She finished her shower regimen by moisturizing her legs and using a hair dryer to blow-dry the area around her chastity device.

Suitably exercised and cleaned she donned her daily maid uniform of black dress, garter belt and stockings, bra and black pumps with five inch stiletto heels. Working makeup consisted of eyeliner, mascara and lipstick. It was Karin's decision when more make-up was warranted.

Suzette's heels clicked along the tile floor as she made her way to the living room. From the book shelf she selected a book suitable for her walking exercise. Just in case someone was watching, or might view a recording later, she turned and curtsied to the camera mounted in the ceiling corner. She carefully placed the book on her head and then let her arms fall slowly to her sides, elbows in, forearms out and wrists hanging limply. Carefully she stepped out, her back straight, taking small steps, one foot in front of the other, heel-toe, heel-toe. She made it to the end of the room and executed a slow and cautious turn, but the book slid from her head. Her reflexes were good; she caught the book and placed it on top of her head. Before starting across the room again she glanced at the mantle clock. *It hasn't even been two minutes, almost, almost twenty eight to go.* Suzette hated these tiresome and monotonous drills, book balancing and curtsey practice. They were mindless and it made it hard to concentrate. And yet Karin seemed to know when she was slacking in her efforts and she was punished. *OK, focus, we need to get this over with – concentrate – balance – posture.* She stepped out again; *back straight, titties out, sissy wrists and sissy steps.*

Sharon leaned over Laurel's shoulder to get a better look at the monitor. "How many times has he dropped the book?"

"Four," Laurel said. "And Ms. Calloway wants us

to call him her, or she."

"Well, her, him, it, she, slut...whatever. With these papers," Sharon held out a black leather portfolio, "she's fucked – big time."

"Yea?"

"Oh yea, once she signs, you witness and I notarize, it's all over. Our little sissy slut's got nothing; Karin's got it covered, signed sealed and delivered." Sharon stood and tucked the portfolio under her arm. "So, go to lunch and then go seal the fate of our former boss?"

Laurel clicked off her computer, "I can't wait."

Suzette feared the daytime doorbell. It was never good news; if it wasn't Miss Trudi it was something equally painful, degrading or humiliating. Karin controlled access to the house so any visitor came with her approval, and must be properly greeted – and obeyed. She jumped at the first ring, but quickly composed herself and walked to the door; *It's probably those papers I was supposed to sign.* Her trepidation was well founded as she opened the door and saw two former employees.

Sharon and Laurel stood at the door. Their faces showed no surprise, having witnessed Suzette's performances on the web-cam feeds at their offices.

"Slut!" Sharon took control, ever the efficient Administrative Supervisor. Shorter than Laurel, and more full-figured, Sharon possessed an authoritative air that must have always given Steven an office thrill. "Are you going to invite us in?"

Suzette executed an automatic bob curtsey. "Yes, sorry Sharon –

The hand hit his face with a resounding SLAP, jerking his head around and sending a clip-on earring flying across the room.

"MISTRESS SHARON," she growled as Sharon pushed past him into the foyer.

Laurel followed behind, unable to control her laughter. "You asked for that one. Best to remember who you and who WE are." She plucked a cane from the umbrella stand as she walked by.

"Yes, Mistress Laurel." His hand stroked his cheek and he stole a glance in the mirror. *She may have given me a black eye.*

Laurel slashed the air with the cane, "Wicked."

"You know how to use that?" Sharon asked.

Laurel giggled and shook her blonde hair, "No."

"On-the-Job training?" Sharon laughed. "Somebody might get hurt."

"You think?"

Suzette quickly turned to follow the women as they went to Karin's home office.

Suzette watched Sharon sit in Karin's desk chair while Laurel relaxed in a wingback chair in the corner, menacingly tapping the cane on the footstool.

Sharon began removing a sheaf of papers from her briefcase. She was focused on organizing the papers and didn't even look at Suzette. "Do you think we might get some drinks? What do you think Laurel, our little slut seems a bit slow in the service area."

"Absolutely, I remember how he – oh, she – used to be when she was our boss: "where's this, get me that, I need –

"Sorry Mistress Sharon, Mistress Laurel – uh – what would you like?" Suzette performed her best and deepest curtsey.

"Coffee," Sharon said.

"Diet Cola," Laurel said. She grabbed a book from a nearby end table, "Over here slut." Laurel waited while Suzette approached and curtsied. "Put this book on your head and keep it there while you bring our refreshments. We watched your efforts earlier and you need practice."

"Yes, Miss Laurel."

"And ice cubes," Sharon finished with her papers. "Bring a bucket of ice cubes."

Both women laughed as Suzette curtsied, placed the book on her head, and carefully walked from the room.

"Can you believe we used to work for that twerp, rush to get his coffee, pull a file or make copies?" Sharon shook her head. "I always felt there was something; I just couldn't put my finger on it."

"I used to catch him looking at my feet," said Laurel, "thought he had a foot or leg fetish, but I think he wanted to wear my shoes." She removed a digital camera from her purse, "Karin said she wanted pictures. I guess the high heel is definitely on the other foot now."

PLOP! Both women smiled at the sound of a book hitting the kitchen floor and the scurrying of stilettos on tile.

Within minutes Suzette appeared. She held a silver try with a coffee service, a Diet Cola and a bucket of ice cubes.

"Turn around, look at me," ordered Laurel. "Ms. Calloway wanted pictures, something about the employee newsletter?"

"Give us your best curtsey," Sharon teased, "hold it, smile and look at the camera."

Suzette did her best to curtsey while holding the tray – and smiling – but the fear and shame were evident. She blinked at the camera flash and almost dropped the tray.

Laurel selected 'play' on the camera to look at the picture. "Perfect, what a total sissy you are. Now serve Sharon her coffee and bend over so we can get a nice view of your cute panties with the ruffles. Oh and be sure and turn to look at the camera. We want everyone to know it's you – Sissy Suzette." The women let Suzette serve each one of them and then ordered Suzette to place the try on a table.

"Over here," Sharon pointed to the floor by her chair. "We need to take care of Ms. Calloway's paper work – before we take care of you." She looked at Laurel. "How many times did he drop the book?"

"Five times on the video and once a few minutes ago."

"Six, very well. Take six ice cubes slut, and stick them up your sissy ass."

For a moment Suzette remained frozen in place, but another stinging SLAP from Sharon had him reaching for the ice cubes.

"Turn around," ordered Sharon, "We want to

watch. Laurel, get some pictures of this. Six, and shove them all the way in your sissy pussy - slut. Face the camera...smile, show everyone how much you like having that little hole filled."

The women laughed and jeered as Suzette gingerly inserted six ice cubes up her ass.

"Cold?" mocked Sharon.

"Y-y-y-es, M-m-m-istress."

"Not our problem. Kneel; you've got papers to sign. You've served us refreshments, now you'll serve up something even more precious for Ms. Calloway, your life."

One by one Sharon handed papers down to the kneeling sissy maid.

"This signs over all your finances and puts all the accounts in Ms. Calloway's name only. This deeds all material possessions to Ms. Calloway, and a General Power of Attorney giving all rights and decisions to Ms. Calloway."

Suzette knelt and tried to sign, but was shaking from her ice-filled ass.

"Too cold?" teased Laurel.

"Yes, Mistress."

"Do you want to take one out?" Her voice now had a more honeyed tone.

"Please, Mistress, yes, oh please."

"OK, one, you may remove one. Squeeze it out; make us a little icy poopsicle."

Suzette reached behind her, squeezed her buttocks and caught the piece of ice in her hand. Her relief was short-lived.

Sharon, squeezed her embossing seal on the first

document. "Put the ice cube in your mouth."

Suzette turned to Sharon, who continued with her paperwork, ignoring the kneeling sissy. "Mistress? You mean –"

The cane landed with a stinging blow, very high on the buttocks. There was the first searing pain, and then that second bloom of deeper pain. Suzette shrieked.

"Put the fucking ice cube in your mouth!" Laurel struck with the cane again, this time leaving a nasty welt on Suzette's shoulder. She drew the cane back for a third blow as Suzette popped the ice cube in her mouth. "That's better. You need to learn to do what you're told. Does your ice cube taste yummy?"

Suzette shook her head, her face showing the distaste of the ice cube, and tears streaming down her cheeks from the wicked cane.

"So the rest of the ice cubes can stay in your ass?"

Defeated, Suzette nodded. She was totally humiliated by women she used to supervise, her sphincter felt frozen and her ass and arm stung from the cane.

Laurel backed up to take another picture, "Look at the camera and smile. Say 'I'm a happy sissy slut'."

"This one is a personal services contract saying that you will provide domestic services for as long as Ms. Calloway deems necessary." Sharon handed down yet another paper and Suzette signed while the camera flash lit up the room.

Six

$\mathcal{K}$arin checked the image in the mirror. The turquoise headband and its complimenting colors went nicely with her red hair and green eyes. She turned sideways and smoothed the fabric over her taught midsection. The matching leotard displayed a supple, yet ample figure. Before heading into the workout area she removed the velvet bag from her locker and shook the contents into her hand. Even in the harsh locker room lighting the gold glittered. She'd selected the faceted cut specifically for that purpose, and not one, but two; it was to be a shiny lure, the bigger the bait, the bigger the catch. Her elegantly manicured hands with the blood red nails fastened both stunning anklets on her right ankle. She sat on the bench, extended her leg and twirled her ankle, pleased with the way the light played of her leg. *Time to troll...for the big ones.*

She'd seldom used the company workout facilities, but now that she was the CEO... It was after business hours, yet there was still a good crowd, many liked to wind down their day with a workout and a steam, and the facilities were free. She started with a few minutes on the Stairmaster, getting the blood flowing and the muscles warmed up. There was the usual banter, 'long day huh, ready for the weekend, feels good to let it out.' She traded quips and salutations easily enough; the gym was a more democratic environment, the great leveler among the corporate masses.

She innocently dabbed at her forehead with the white cotton towel. Her gaze, however, was focused on the man at the squat rack. He was clearly the biggest man in the room, not bulky, but well muscled, with that hard strong, All-American Tight End body. The fifteen years out of college hadn't seemed to have put an extra pound or ounce of fat on him.

Brent Saunders, six-foot five; as the Corporate Trainer he easily took command of a room. Despite his powerful physical presence he had the ability to put people at ease, yet retain total control. Karin smiled, *He's reputed to be quite the ladies man.*

She moved across the room, exchanging a few pleasantries here and there, accepting condolences about Steven's 'breakdown' and compliments on how well she had stepped in to fill the breach as CEO. Karin though about the pictures: Suzette serving coffee to Sharon, stuffing ice cubes up his ass, kneeling and signing his life away. *Steven is gone; say hello to Sissy Maid Suzette.*

The bench press machine, not far from the squat rack, was her destination. She dropped her towel over the handles and then fiddled, rather loudly, with the weight adjustment mechanism. Before she heard him, or felt his touch, she felt his presence; there was something about him...

"Need some help?" His hand touched her shoulder, gently, but it sent a pulse through her.

"I'm not used to this machine."

"Let me help you." His voice was smooth and rich, like an aged Cognac, and his eyes had the same deep amber color. "Lay down and scoot back until your hands are under the grips – a little more – good."

She licked her lips: an invitation, to make them shine? "I didn't want to take you away from your workout."

"No problem, I finished the squats, today I'm doing legs and back. You ever work on this machine?"

"No, I usually work out elsewhere, but since I'm back at the company."

"Yea, I'm sorry about Steven, the breakdown and all. He didn't seem like the type – if you know what I mean."

"Thank you, yes, it's all been rather hard on him."

"He hired me; Steven was the one who brought me into the company. I hope you're doing OK, if there's ever anything I can do..."

"Thank you," Karin's eyes met his, "I'll certainly keep that in mind."

Brent studied the woman prone below him, the face slightly flushed, the wisps of scarlet hair peeking out from the headband, and those emerald green eyes. "OK, we'll start easy – and work our way up."

Karin pushed up on the handles and felt his hands lightly below hers.

"All right, hold it at the top for a second and slowly let it down."

As she let the handles descend she thrust out her chest, the movement made even more pronounced as her elbows lowered. Her nipples strained against the thin Lycra top, and she saw that Mr. Brent Saunders was taking it all in.

"Good, good, let's try a couple more and then we'll do some negative reps."

They repeated the most sensuous chest press ever performed in the company gym, both working up a sweat from the 'intensity'.

"Here, I'm gonna add more weight and lift it up for you and you s-l-o-w-l-y let it back down. These are negative reps."

The weight was, indeed, heavier, and it made even more demands on Karin. When she was finished she sat up, took the towel offered by Brent and dabbed at her face. She dropped the towel in her lap and slowly ran her hands over her breasts, "Yes, oh – I can feel that exercise, here – and here." She extended her right leg. "What about calves, can you recommend something to help my calves – so I look sexy in my highest heels?"

"I'd never imagine you wearing really high heels? Aren't you actually taller than Steven."

She continued to move her ankle in small circles, the faceted, gold chains casting their 'come hither' gleam. "I'm five eight, Steven is five seven. But I like to wear heels and Steven didn't mind me being taller. I bet that's a problem you never had." She ran a finger down his chest. "We could wear our highest heels and still feel like we're with a real man with you."

He pulled her hand to his lips and gave it a little

kiss. "The calf machine is over here." He led her to the machine, never releasing her hand. "Sit down; slide your knees under the pads."

Brent took her through a calf workout, his eyes paying special attention to the gold anklets. When they were through he escorted her to the juice bar.

"Thank you for the help." She wrapped her lips seductively around a straw. "I enjoyed it."

"My pleasure, I noticed your anklets."

She held up her leg, pointed her toe and gave the lithesome limb a shake. "You like?"

"Very much; do you know what it means, to some people? Wearing an anklet on the right ankle?

She pulled off her headband, shook her hair and licked her lips. "Why don't you explain it to me – over drinks and dinner?"

"I'm wondering if Steven really had a breakdown." Brent leaned over to refill Karin's wine glass, "Although you seem in need of consoling...of some sort."

Beneath the table, the pointed toe of Karin's high heel traced a line up his leg. "I have...needs...yes." She rubbed the heel against his leg, using the leverage to slide her foot from the shoe. Her foot snaked up his leg, and into his crotch, her toes exploring – and feeling his reaction. "Mmm, needs you seem to be able to fill."

He signaled the waiter for a Scotch. "I'll do whatever I can for you – and the company."

"Will you – really? I'll see if I have any openings you can fill."

Karin picked up her cigarette case and Bent was ready with a light.

"Yes, you seem most capable."

Brent returned the lighter to his pocket and took a sip of Scotch. "Tell me about Steven. Are you getting a divorce?"

"Not," she chuckled, "in the conventional sense. But our relationship has changed."

"He didn't have a breakdown?"

"Oh, he did; I saw to that, orchestrated it, and watched it happen. And now, I own him – and the company. It's all mine." She gave him an appraising look, weighing how much to reveal. *Are the things they say about him true?* "People, certain people, say you have a reputation"

He sat back, toyed with his drink, and watched the ravishing redhead finish her cigarette. "I help wives – and husbands – when they need it."

"A specialist of sorts? I understand that – and appreciate it. And would you help me?"

He leaned in, a smile creeping across his lips. "You need a Bull? You want to cuckold Steven?"

"I want what I want, when I want it. And right now that means you in my bed. Steven will do what he's told. He's…changed…different."

"Changed? How?"

"Come home with me…you'll see." She picked up her cell phone and placed a call. Her sudden and harsh tone intrigued Brent. "I'm coming home, with a friend, be ready for us, dressed – and ready to serve."

Suzette closed the cell phone and literally ran to her room. She was surprised, and yet not, by this sudden visitation by another outsider. First it had been Sharon and Laurel, and now Mistress Karin was bringing home someone else...a man, a woman? In her room she quickly put on her stockings, maid's dress and heels. Mistress hadn't given very detailed instructions, but Suzette left nothing to chance and added the long earrings and heavy makeup that Mistress preferred on her slut.

A quick house cleaning was in order and Suzette grabbed her feather duster and attacked all the likely flat surfaces that a visitor may encounter. She double-checked the refrigerator to ensure that chilled white wine, one of Mistress's favorites, and Champagne were available.

The sound of the car in the driveway and the automatic garage door opener signaled that Mistress and her guest had arrived.

The footfalls that resounded through the foyer sent a chill through Suzette. She recognized the distinctive clicks of Mistress's designer heels, but the other steps had the heavy sound of a male.

Suzette was waiting, and when they entered the room she gave her best curtsey.

"Sweet, isn't she?" Karin said.

"So this is what happened to Steven – interesting."

Brent's arm snaked around Karin and pulled her to him.

Karin didn't resist, and let her body melt into his. She felt his warmth, his strength, his authority. "You don't seem surprised."

"No, not at all, I've seen others, many others." Still holding Karin close he circled the nervous sissy maid. "I've seen some with breast implants, reconstructive surgery, undergoing hormonal therapy. Yours has potential."

Suzette's stomach knotted to her about being discussed as if she were some experiment. She was on display, being observed…evaluated.

"Yes, much potential here Karin; he never was very tall was he? And I don't ever remember him wearing a beard or moustache."

"No, it's quite easy to keep him hairless, and you're right, I've always been taller." She snuggled closer to Brent and looked up at him. "It's nice to be able to wear heels and still look up at a man."

Her words were like a dagger to Suzette's heart, but in spite of it all her flaccid cock was trying to erect in its plastic cage. *I'm a cuckold – and a sissy maid.*

Brent pulled Karin in front of him, his massive chest pressed into her back. His strong hands traced a line down her hips and then back up to cup her breasts. "Lift up your dress," he ordered Suzette.

Suzette daintily grabbed the hem of her black maid's dress and lifted it up. Both Karin and Brent laughed at the sight of the pitiful sissy cock trying to erect.

"It turns her on," purred Karin, "to see me in the

arms of a real man...and enjoying it."

Brent's fingers gently settled on Karin's nipples; when he squeezed - she sighed. He bent down to whisper in her ear, but not so quietly that Suzette couldn't hear every word. "It would be my distinct honor to make him an official cuckold."

"Cream pies and all?" Karin teased.

"The first of many."

Suzette trembled with fear and excitement and felt the drool of sissy pre-cum fall from her chastity device onto her stocking.

END

NOW AVAILABLE

What can be better than a Mistress and her submissive male? How about two Mistresses and their submissive males - and their Alpha Male friends? What happens when Karin meets and mentors Joanna? It surely can't be good for their hapless maids, Suzette and Donna. Fun will be had by all, or maybe not. Follow the further adventures of Dominant Women and their submissive males in:

"YES, I READ THE BOOKS, MISTRESS KARIN AND THE BREAKING CAGE, AND I THOUGHT...WHY NOT? WHY SHOULD I BE BOTHERED WITH HOUSEWORK, SHOPPING, ERRANDS, LAUNDRY AND ALL THE REST?

"LOVERS, WHY SHOULDN'T I HAVE THEM WHEN-EVER I WANT? AND NOW I DO. IT'S ALL ABOUT ME...AND I COULDN'T BE HAPPIER!

"HIM? I THINK HE'S, OR SHE'S, HAPPIER TOO. THE CHASTITY MAKES HIM SO DOCILE AND SUBMISSIVE. HE'S BECOME A WONDERFUL HOUSEKEEPER AND ALL MY LOVERS THINK HE'S THE CUTEST LITTLE THING.

"HE'S IN THE KITCHEN NOW, THE PERFECT LITTLE SISSY MAID WIFE, PROPERLY DRESSED IN HIS WIFEY DRESS, APRON AND HEELS. HE'S MAKING MASTER'S FAVORITE POT ROAST. IT ALWAYS GETS HIM EXCITED TO SERVE MASTER AND I AT ONE OF OUR ROMANTIC DINNERS.

"REALLY, DIANE, YOU NEED TO MAKE CARL INTO A SISSY MAID. FROM LAZY HUSBAND TO PRODUCTIVE SISSY MAID, IT'S A MOVE YOU WON'T REGRET !"

The Breaking Cage

by

Constance Pennington Smythe

Karin Calloway relaxed in her chair and absently turned the pages of a magazine as the warm water and heated stones in the footbath soaked away the stresses of her day. Scents of vanilla and lavender filled the air; sconces on the wall gave the room a muted amber glow. The New Age music in the background, harps and flutes, that was something she could do without. Some vintage Sinatra, Old Blue Eyes with the Nelson Riddle Orchestra, or maybe even some Harry Connick Jr. would be more to her liking; elegant and classy as herself.

She watched a petite spa technician in a too-tight, too-short white dress administer a pedicure to another customer. She'd noted the girl's name badge, Tammy, when she'd started the footbath. Karin's eyes couldn't help but linger on the taut fabric as it stretched over those young, firm hips. *VPL, a fashion no-no, but there's something about her.*

The woman receiving Tammy's attentions was close to Karin's age and quite striking. Their eyes met when Karin entered the room and they exchanged polite smiles and nods in silent greeting. Then they both went back to their magazines and moments of selfish indulgence and pampering.

"Almost finished, Ma'am, your feet didn't need that much work. You're very fortunate to have a husband who takes care of them," Tammy said.

Karin raised her eyes and glanced over the top of her magazine, intrigued by the conversation.

Tammy turned to Karin. "I'll be right with you Ms. Calloway." She gathered up her things and prepared to move to Karin when the other woman spoke.

"Tammy!"

Tammy turned to face her client, who silently pointed to her feet.

Karin dropped the magazine, her terrycloth robe enfolding the pages. Something was going to happen and she didn't want to miss it.

Tammy stepped before her customer, knelt and reverently placed a tender kiss on the top of each foot. She released the feet and looked up to see the woman smiling down at her, but silently demanding more. Tammy picked up the pan of water from the footbath, brought it to her lips and took a drink, her pink tongue licking the residue from her lips. The woman in the chair nodded approvingly. The ritual act of obeisance completed, Tammy rose, set the pan on a shelf and gathered her things. She cast an embarrassed look at Karin, "I'll be right with you Ms. Calloway."

Karin's eyes followed Tammy as she left, then she turned her gaze to the woman across the room.

The woman rose, tightened her robe, and walked to Karin. "I hope I didn't shock you".

Karin smiled and shrugged her shoulders, "actually, not at all."

"Really? Some would be shocked at such an overt and submissive display."

Karin's green eyes narrowed and she pursed her lips as if to consider. "Some would, ones who don't understand the desperate needs and nature of those who would be submissive. She said your husband does your feet?"

"Yes, quite well in fact. But I also enjoy the pampering here. And," she said, casting her eyes to the door, "Tammy is such a treasure."

"I quite agree, she is - special," Karin said, extending a hand. "My name is Karin Calloway."

"Joanna, Joanna Barnes," said the other woman, taking Karin's hand and smiling. "We really must get together."

Joanna added cream to her coffee. "I've not seen you at the spa before."

Karin dabbed at her lips with a napkin and returned it to the table. "Yes, I usually go to Giovanni's, but they're remodeling. Based on the performance of your lovely little Tammy I may consider switching locations. You noticed her submissive nature right off?"

"Not immediately, but even at the first appointment there was definitely something about the way she touched my feet, almost a - reverence."

Karin nodded. "Not surprising, someone with a

strong submissive need couldn't help but exhibit some of that on the job, kneeling, giving pedicures, serving and waiting. She probably chose that vocation specifically for those reasons. How far have you taken her?"

"Only what you witnessed, foot kissing and drinking my footbath."

"Still, it makes for a wonderfully entertaining afternoon."

"Most entertaining."

Karin leaned back and considered her next question. "You said your husband does your feet. Is he submissive?"

"He likes to be dominated." Joanna paused, unsure how much to reveal to her new-found friend. "Get tied up and spanked. It was a bit of a shock at first, but as I got more comfortable with it I began to see it in more places. I saw the same look in Tammy's eyes that I'd seen in my husband's and out of curiosity I pushed it to see how far she'd go. I enjoy it: the power of having someone submit to me."

"How far have you gone with your husband?"

"Some bondage, foot kissing, he's bought crops, whips and paddles that I use on him."

"Uh-huh, sounds typical." Karin studied Joanna for a moment and leaned forward; here was new blood, a potential convert to the sisterhood. "How far would you like it to go?"

Joanna shrugged, having never considered the question. "I don't know. How far is there - to go, I mean?"

Karin's lips curled into a demonic smile, time to seal another submissive's fate. "All the way, complete submission to you, 24/7, or whenever you desire, complete service, absolute obedience. Admittedly it's not for everyone, but there can be some advantages - for you."

"I'm not sure." Joanna drummed her nails on the table nervously. "I can't imagine what that would be like. Even if it's something that I wanted – I mean; would Gary want to go that far?"

"That's your first mistake..." Karin settled back in her chair allowing Joanna some space. "...allowing him a choice in the matter."

Joanna hesitated. "I don't know, up until now it's been..."

"Would you like to see how it can be, how far it can go?"

Joanna silently nodded.

"Come see me on Friday...alone."

"SEE, WHAT DID I TELL YOU?"

"HE'S ACTUALLY ON HIS KNEES, CRAWLING TO US."

"WELCOME MISS SIMONE PROPERLY, KISS HER FEET."

"HE'S REALLY DOING IT, HE'S KISSING MY FEET!"

"THAT'S ONLY A SAMPLE. HE'LL DO WHATEVER HE'S TOLD. HE'S QUITE OBEDIENT, QUITE WELL-TRAINED. PUT YOUR HANDS ON THE FLOOR. NOW BEG SIMONE TO STEP ON YOUR HANDS WITH HER HIGH HEELS."

"OH I LIKE THIS, I CAN FEEL HIS HANDS UNDER-NEATH MY FEET. FEEL THAT, BITCH!"

"GO AHEAD YOU CAN DO IT HARDER, HE'S NOT EVEN CRYING YET."

COMING SOON

Coming in 2008, the third book in the Karin series: ***Weekend With Friends.*** The circle of Dominant Women grows as Joanna introduces her friend Simone to the advantages of chastised, submissive, sissy maids. Joanna invites friend Simone and her husband Scott for the weekend, and Gary is outed as sissy maid Donna, and spends the weekend as a sex toy.

Weekend With Friends

by

Constance Pennington Smythe

"He really does anything you say?" Simone asked incredulously.

Joanna nodded and smiled, slowly drawing out her reply, "Anything."

The two friends and work colleagues were enjoying a glass of wine on a Friday evening. As they drank they discussed men and relationships, the talk becoming bawdier as the grape was consumed, in vino veritas.

"Yes, he's been my total submissive for quite some time now. I am the Goddess and he is my slave. I am a woman of total leisure and supreme head of the house."

Joanna made the statement matter-of-factly.

Simone took another sip of wine and placed her glass on the table. "Damn, no wonder your house is so clean and you have all this free time. You make him do everything?"

"Actually I really don't have to 'make' him do much at all. At this point, he's so pussy-whipped I only 'make' him do things to see him squirm. But it is fun to try to find new ways to push his buttons."

"What about sex?" Simone asked.

"Hell, I get as much as I want, when I want it, the way I want it, although it's almost never penetrative sex, at least from him. No, I'm afraid his little 'thing' has pretty much been reduced to an implement of torment and frustration for him."

Simone shook her head in amazement.

"I've got his little wanker under lock and key," Joanna continued. "I really don't need it and he can't get to it."

"You don't!" Simone said.

Joanna smiled, reached into her purse and fished out a small key on a golden chain. She held it out to Simone. "If I dangled this in front of Gary he'd be down on his knees in a second, waiting to do whatever I demand."

Simone shook her head in disbelief and drank the rest of her wine. "Really?"

Joanna nodded, "Really."

Simone cautiously eyed Joanna and leaned in closer. "So, uh, what kinds of things do you, uh, do - exactly."

Joanna laughed. "Shit, Simone. Don't you ever cruise stuff on the web, read Variations, Penthouse

Letters, play little sex games?"

Simone shifted nervously in her chair. "Well, yea, I mean, Scott and I have seen some videos and sometimes he buys these magazines and, and - I mean damn, Joanna; you're talking the real shit, right?"

Joanna narrowed her eyes over the top of her wine glass and deliberately nodded at her friend.

Simone sat back in her chair and sighed. *What's this all about? Where is this all going?* Another question obviously on her mind, she studied Joanna. "So, are you like, a, a Dominatrix?"

Joanna reached into her purse for a silver cigarette case and languidly placed a cigarillo in a holder. "If you're asking me if I dress up in leather and high-heeled boots and carry a whip and a riding crop, yes. If you're asking me if I put Gary in bondage and beat him, yes. If you're asking if I fuck him in the ass with a strap-on and put nipple clamps on him, yes."

Simone stared, wide-eyed.

Joanna took a drag from her cigarette and expelled a sensuous stream of smoke. "The idea excites you, doesn't it?"

Simone leaned back as if trying to maintain some space from Joanna. "Well, I mean, yeah. I never really knew any body that actually did that kind of stuff, or at least admitted to it."

Joanna reclined in her chair and studied her friend. There was a moment of awkward silence while Simone played with her wine glass and Joanna finished her cigarillo.

Joanna leaned forward and purred, "Would you like to see it? Would you like to watch Gary submit to us, to crawl and kiss our feet?"

Simone felt the wetness in her sex; the idea did excite her. Hell, Scott read his damned porno mags and sometimes they rented 'fuck-me-suck-me' videos, but sex didn't seem to be as exciting these last few years. Yet, here was her friend Joanna, a good ten years older, and having a great sex life; a life that Simone could not imagine. *Yea, why not* she thought, *what's the harm in just checking it out?* Simone tried to be nonchalant, "Sure, I'd like that sometime."

Joanna cocked her head, "Now?" she asked.

Simone lost her composed façade. "What, you mean now? Tonight?"

Joanna shrugged her shoulders in a 'why not' gesture.

Simone felt warm. Was it the wine or the steamy topic of conversation? The kids were out doing some Friday night activity and Scott was off doing who knows what. She was out with Joanna because she had the early part of the evening free, so why not? She regained her composure enough to say, "Yes, Joanna, I'd be very interested to see what you are up to. You surprise me, you really do surprise me."

Joanna reached across the table, smiled and reassuringly took Simone's hand. "You won't regret this. It will be fun." She signaled the cute young waiter for the check.

COMING in 2008

Female Domination Short Stories

By

Constance Pennington Smythe

It's the first collection of Female Domination short stories published by erotic author Constance Pennington Smythe. Enjoy the powerful and erotic world of Female Domination and male submission with these new stories and favorite themes: Chastity, Cuckolding, Mini Men, Suburb Submissions and more, all with Dominant Women and the submissive men in their lives.

Turn the page for a preview of A Visit to Smythe Stables, just one of the many offerings to be found in this new work.

A Visit
To
Smythe Stables

Welcome to Smythe Stables
A Division of
Smythe Domination, Ltd.

Tours and milking parties by appointment only.
Family visits by appointment only.
Pony cart races every Saturday.

Visit our gift shop complete with a wide array of
milking videos and milking accessories.

Custom-made milking videos of your husband,
boyfriend or son available.

Ask about our sissy cream delivery service. Fresh
spunk delivered to you daily to use in feeding your
sissy maids.

Note:
Males are forbidden to walk upright.
Males may only speak when spoken to.
Do not feed the males.
Males do not have names, only numbers.
Please DO handle the males.

by
Constance Pennington Smythe

A Visit
To
Smythe Stables

Chapter ONE

The gravel crunched under the tires as the black and white chartered bus, its tinted windows hiding the occupants inside, made its way up the winding drive. Passing a green fenced in pasture and a wooded area it slowed to a stop in front of the imposing red and white building. It was a long, low and windowless structure with several sliding doors along one side; the sign in the front, Smythe Stables, was the only clue as to what might be inside. With a hiss, the doors of the bus folded open.

A tall austere woman rose from her seat at the front of the bus and turned to face her young charges. Her height was enhanced by the gleaming black stilettos, and the long, sheer nylon covered legs that extended from her black leather pencil skirt. She moved effortlessly on the wicked high heels as she walked down the aisle of the bus. Looking back at her were row after row of feminine faces, this year's graduating class from Lady Caroline's Academy for Young Ladies.

"Today is the practical exercise in the milking of the submissive male. We've covered the theory and physiology in the classroom. Here you will put the theory into practice. Your future husbands will need to be regularly milked. Whether or not you do this or assign it to someone else, it is important to knowledge of the practice. It is my recommendation that either you, or your Alpha Male lover perform this service on your husband. Such personal 'attention' is more humiliating to the male and drives them further into submission. Ms Constance Pennington Smythe has made her milking stable available to us, very generous of her. She will host an afternoon tea for us at her club, and then we will return to the stables for the strap-on exercises before we depart. Are there any questions?"

A beautiful girl with flowing blond hair raised her hand. She was dressed in the same uniform as her classmates: a crisp white blouse, sheer stockings, bracelet-length kid leather gloves, a tartan mini skirt and high-heeled court shoes. "Where do all the males inside come from?"

Lady Caroline slipped on her black leather suit coat. "Disciplinary problems, males who couldn't be trained or perform to standards. A few languish here simply because their owners tired of them and at least here they can serve some function." She turned to look at a pretty brunette. "Susan, I believe your father is inside."

Susan smiled and nodded. "Mother sold him to Ms Smythe. He was getting in the way, wasn't good for sex, a premature ejaculator Mom said, and wasn't making a good domestic. We have a really good sissy maid now and Miguel is a better lover for Mom."

The girl in the seat in front of Susan turned around. "Your Dad's in there? That's fuckin' cool."

Her outburst brought instant recrimination from Lady Caroline. "Deidre, mind your language!"

"Yes, Ma'am."

"Remember girls, domination and superiority are not crass; wield your power and authority in a regal and ladylike manner. When we go inside you will each pick out a slave. Warders will be around to provide you with gloves and lubricant and show you how to hook the suction nipple to their penis. The males have not been milked for several days so should be very amenable to our attention. But to help them along everyone add a spritz of scent."

Twenty five gloved hands disappeared into twenty five identical and fashionable clutches to remove bottles of expensive perfume. In an instant the bus filled with a sensual aroma.

The male bus driver, naked and gagged with a large penis gag, breathed in the heady scent and felt his cock try to stiffen in its chastity cage. The sharp spikes inside the device brought immediate pain and put down any attempts at erection.

Caroline returned to the front of the bus. "When you get inside, remember YOU are the superior Female. This is your last semester at my academy. You're all of legal and marriageable age and when you graduate you will enter the world to search out and cull those submissive males from the herd. It won't be difficult. Society abounds with them, and I and my faculty have provided you all the skills and tools you need to capture a husband and to staff your house-holds with sissy maids. But to obtain maximum efficiency from male slaves you need to know about their care and feeding. So pay attention today, these are valuable lessons. Please form up outside the bus and wait for me."

The girls walked down the aisle, each one stopping to tighten their leather gloved hand into a fist and deliver a hard blow to the bus driver's right arm and shoulder. His arm was covered in black, blue and greenish bruises that never healed. Chained to his seat there was no way he could escape, even if he wanted to. But he'd accepted this for so long that although they hurt, he sat and took his beatings, offering whimpers of pain into his penis gag. The girls, for their part, delighted in seeing who could force the loudest wails from his gagged mouth.

Caroline watched this ritual with amused detachment. *At this rate he'll only be good for another year before that right arm is useless. Oh well, I'll sell him to Constance and he can spend the rest of his days inside the stables.* Before leaving the bus she took the remote control from her pocket and pressed "medium." The steel balls inside the driver's butt plug began to gyrate and bounce against one another. She smiled as the driver squirmed at the anal invasion. Grabbing his wrists she brought them to his neck, locking the cuffs to his collar.

He looked at her; his eyes begging and pleading for mercy. He knew there was no mercy, never had been, never would be. But something deep inside of him still searched for what he knew he'd never find.

She saw the look, reached down and viciously pinched a nipple. *Eventually that look will be gone; he'll be destroyed, resigned to his fate. But I do like them like this, ever hopeful...right before they're completely broken.*

She left the bus and joined her fresh-faced entourage: so prim, so proper, so perfectly dressed and coifed. And so full of malevolent evil, carefully inculcated by her, "Follow me girls."

About the Author

Constance Pennington Smythe

Constance Pennington Smythe is an erotic author and also a writer of mainstream works under another name. She has lived abroad, been an adjunct professor, possesses a Graduate degree, and speaks another language.

www.cpsmythe.com